Henry James OM (15 April 1843 – 28 February 1916) was an American-British author regarded as a key transitional figure between literary realism and literary modernism, and is considered by many to be among the greatest novelists in the English language. He was the son of Henry James Sr. and the brother of renowned philosopher and psychologist William James and diarist Alice James.

He is best known for a number of novels dealing with the social and marital interplay between émigré Americans, English people, and continental Europeans. Examples of such novels include The Portrait of a Lady, The Ambassadors, and The Wings of the Dove. His later works were increasingly experimental. In describing the internal states of mind and social dynamics of his characters, James often made use of a style in which ambiguous or contradictory motives and impressions were overlaid or juxtaposed in the discussion of a character's psyche.(Source: Wikipedia)

Literary works:
Watch and Ward (1871)
Roderick Hudson (1875)
The American (1877)
The Europeans (1878)
Confidence (1879)
Washington Square (1880)
The Portrait of a Lady (1881)
The Bostonians (1886)
The Princess Casamassima (1886)
The Reverberator (1888)
The Tragic Muse (1890)
The Other House (1896)
The Spoils of Poynton (1897)
What Maisie Knew (1897)

A PASSIONATE PILGRIM

HENRY JAMES

PRINCE CLASSICS

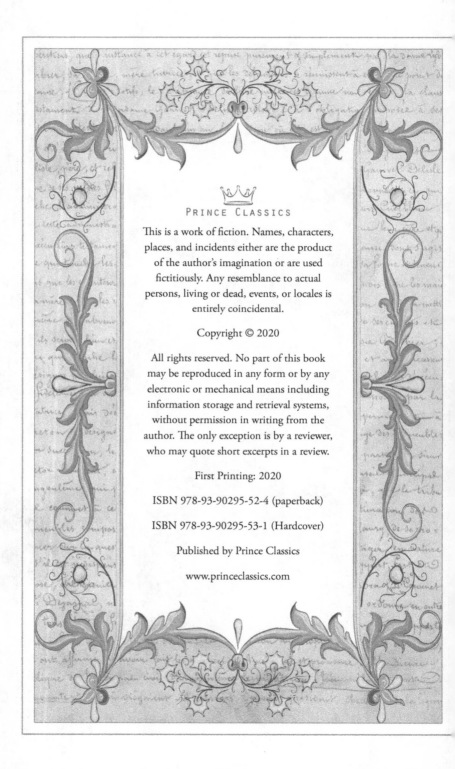

First Printing: 2020

ISBN 978-93-90295-52-4 (paperback)

ISBN 978-93-90295-53-1 (Hardcover)

Published by Prince Classics

www.princeclassics.com

Contents

A
PASSIONATE
PILGRIM

I

Intending to sail for America in the early part of June, I determined to spend the interval of six weeks in England, to which country my mind's eye only had as yet been introduced. I had formed in Italy and France a resolute preference for old inns, considering that what they sometimes cost the ungratified body they repay the delighted mind. On my arrival in London, therefore, I lodged at a certain antique hostelry, much to the east of Temple Bar, deep in the quarter that I had inevitably figured as the Johnsonian. Here, on the first evening of my stay, I descended to the little coffee-room and bespoke my dinner of the genius of "attendance" in the person of the solitary waiter. No sooner had I crossed the threshold of this retreat than I felt I had cut a golden-ripe crop of English "impressions." The coffee-room of the Red Lion, like so many other places and things I was destined to see in the motherland, seemed to have been waiting for long years, with just that sturdy sufferance of time written on its visage, for me to come and extract the romantic essence of it.

The latent preparedness of the American mind even for the most characteristic features of English life was a matter I meanwhile failed to get to the bottom of. The roots of it are indeed so deeply buried in the soil of our early culture that, without some great upheaval of feeling, we are at a loss to say exactly when and where and how it begins. It makes an American's enjoyment of England an emotion more searching than anything Continental. I had seen the coffee-room of the Red Lion years ago, at home—at Saragossa Illinois—in books, in visions, in dreams, in Dickens, in Smollett, in Boswell. It was small and subdivided into six narrow compartments by a series of perpendicular screens of mahogany, something higher than a man's stature, furnished on either side with a meagre uncushioned ledge, denominated in ancient Britain a seat. In each of these rigid receptacles was a narrow table—a table expected under stress to accommodate no less than four pairs of active British elbows. High pressure indeed had passed away from the Red Lion for ever. It now knew only that of memories and ghosts and atmosphere. Round the room there marched, breast-high, a magnificent panelling of mahogany so dark with time and so polished with unremitted friction that by gazing a while into its lucid blackness I made out the dim reflexion of a party of wigged gentlemen in knee-breeches just arrived from York by the coach. On the dark yellow walls, coated by the fumes of English coal, of English mutton of Scotch whiskey, were a dozen melancholy prints, sallow-toned with age—the Derby favourite of the year 1807, the Bank of England, her Majesty the Queen. On the floor was a Turkey carpet—as old as the mahogany almost, as the Bank of England, as the Queen—into which the waiter had in his lonely revolutions trodden so many massive soot-flakes and drops of overflowing beer that the glowing looms of Smyrna would certainly not have recognised it. To say that I ordered my dinner of this archaic type would be altogether to misrepresent the process owing to which, having dreamed of lamb and spinach and a salade de saison, I sat down in penitence to a mutton-chop and a rice pudding. Bracing my feet against the cross-beam of my little oaken table, I opposed to the mahogany partition behind me the vigorous dorsal resistance that must have expressed the old-English idea of repose. The sturdy screen refused even to creak, but my poor Yankee joints made up the deficiency.

While I was waiting there for my chop there came into the room a person whom, after I had looked at him a moment, I supposed to be a fellow lodger and probably the only one. He seemed, like myself, to have submitted to proposals for dinner; the table on the other side of my partition had been prepared to receive him. He walked up to the fire, exposed his back to it and after consulting his watch, looked directly out of the window and indirectly at me. He was a man of something less than middle age and more than middle stature, though indeed you would have called him neither young nor tall. He was chiefly remarkable for his emphasised leanness. His hair, very thin on the summit of his head, was dark short and fine. His eye was of a pale turbid grey, unsuited, perhaps, to his dark hair and well-drawn brows, but not altogether out of harmony with his colourless bilious complexion. His nose was aquiline and delicate; beneath it his moustache languished much rather than bristled. His mouth and chin were negative, or at the most provisional; not vulgar, doubtless, but ineffectually refined. A cold fatal gentlemanly weakness was expressed indeed in his attenuated person. His eye was restless and deprecating; his whole physiognomy, his manner of shifting his weight from foot to foot, the spiritless droop of his head, told of exhausted intentions, of a will relaxed. His dress was neat and "toned down"—he might have been in mourning. I made up my mind on three points: he was a bachelor, he was out of health, he was not indigenous to the soil. The waiter approached him, and they conversed in accents barely audible. I heard the words "claret," "sherry" with a tentative inflexion, and finally "beer" with its last letter changed to "ah." Perhaps he was a Russian in reduced circumstances; he reminded me slightly of certain sceptical cosmopolite Russians whom I had met on the Continent. While in my extravagant way I followed this train—for you see I was interested—there appeared a short brisk man with reddish-brown hair, with a vulgar nose, a sharp blue eye and a red beard confined to his lower jaw and chin. My putative Russian, still in possession of the rug, let his mild gaze stray over the dingy ornaments of the room. The other drew near, and his umbrella dealt a playful poke at the concave melancholy waistcoat. "A penny ha'penny for your thoughts!"

My friend, as I call him, uttered an exclamation, stared, then laid his two hands on the other's shoulders. The latter looked round at me keenly, compassing me in a momentary glance. I read in its own vague light that this was a transatlantic eyebeam; and with such confidence that I hardly needed to see its owner, as he prepared, with his companion, to seat himself at the table adjoining my own, take from his overcoat-pocket three New York newspapers and lay them beside his plate. As my neighbours proceeded to dine I felt the crumbs of their conversation scattered pretty freely abroad. I could hear almost all they said, without straining to catch it, over the top of the partition that divided us. Occasionally their voices dropped to recovery of discretion, but the mystery pieced itself together as if on purpose to entertain me. Their speech was pitched in the key that may in English air be called alien in spite of a few coincidences. The voices were American, however, with a difference; and I had no hesitation in assigning the softer and clearer sound to the pale thin gentleman, whom I decidedly preferred to his comrade. The latter began to question him about his voyage.

"Horrible, horrible! I was deadly sick from the hour we left New York."

"Well, you do look considerably reduced," said the second-comer.

"Reduced! I've been on the verge of the grave. I haven't slept six hours for three weeks." This was said with great gravity.

"Well, I've made the voyage for the last time."

"The plague you have! You mean to locate here permanently?"

"Oh it won't be so very permanent!"

There was a pause; after which: "You're the same merry old boy, Searle. Going to give up the ghost to-morrow, eh?"

"I almost wish I were."

"You're not so sweet on England then? I've heard people say at home that you dress and talk and act like an Englishman. But I know these people here and I know you. You're not one of this crowd, Clement Searle, not you. You'll go under here, sir; you'll go under as sure as my name's Simmons."

Following this I heard a sudden clatter as of the drop of a knife and fork. "Well, you're a delicate sort of creature, if it IS your ugly name! I've been wandering about all day in this accursed city, ready to cry with homesickness and heartsickness and every possible sort of sickness, and thinking, in the absence of anything better, of meeting you here this evening and of your uttering some sound of cheer and comfort and giving me some glimmer of hope. Go under? Ain't I under now? I can't do more than get under the ground!"

Mr. Simmons's superior brightness appeared to flicker a moment in this gust of despair, but the next it was burning steady again. "DON'T 'cry,' Searle," I heard him say. "Remember the waiter. I've grown Englishman enough for that. For heaven's sake don't let's have any nerves. Nerves won't do anything for you here. It's best to come to the point. Tell me in three words what you expect of me."

I heard another movement, as if poor Searle had collapsed in his chair. "Upon my word, sir, you're quite inconceivable. You never got my letter?"

"Yes, I got your letter. I was never sorrier to get anything in my life."

At this declaration Mr. Searle rattled out an oath, which it was well perhaps that I but partially heard. "Abijah Simmons," he then cried, "what demon of perversity possesses you? Are you going to betray me here in a foreign land, to turn out a false friend, a heartless rogue?"

"Go on, sir," said sturdy Simmons. "Pour it all out. I'll wait till you've done. Your beer's lovely," he observed independently to the waiter. "I'll have some more."

"For God's sake explain yourself!" his companion appealed.

There was a pause, at the end of which I heard Mr. Simmons set down his empty tankard with emphasis. "You poor morbid mooning man," he resumed, "I don't want to say anything to make you feel sore. I regularly pity you. But you must allow that you've acted more like a confirmed crank than a member of our best society—in which every one's so sensible."

Mr. Searle seemed to have made an effort to compose himself. "Be so good as to tell me then what was the meaning of your letter."

"Well, you had got on MY nerves, if you want to know, when I wrote it. It came of my always wishing so to please folks. I had much better have let you alone. To tell you the plain truth I never was so horrified in my life as when I found that on the strength of my few kind words you had come out here to seek your fortune."

"What then did you expect me to do?"

"I expected you to wait patiently till I had made further enquiries and had written you again."

"And you've made further enquiries now?"

"Enquiries! I've committed assaults."

"And you find I've no claim?"

"No claim that one of THESE big bugs will look at. It struck me at first that you had rather a neat little case. I confess the look of it took hold of me—"

"Thanks to your liking so to please folks!" Mr. Simmons appeared for a moment at odds with something; it proved to be with his liquor. "I rather think your beer's too good to be true," he said to the waiter. "I guess I'll take water. Come, old man," he resumed, "don't challenge me to the arts of debate, or you'll have me right down on you, and then you WILL feel me. My native sweetness, as I say, was part of it. The idea that if I put the thing through it would be a very pretty feather in my cap and a very pretty penny in my purse was part of it. And the satisfaction of seeing a horrid low American walk right into an old English estate was a good deal of it. Upon my word, Searle, when I think of it I wish with all my heart that, extravagant vain man as you are, I COULD, for the charm of it, put you through! I should hardly care what you did with the blamed place when you got it. I could leave you alone to turn it into Yankee notions—into ducks and drakes as they call 'em here. I should like to see you tearing round over it and kicking up its sacred dust in their very faces!"

"You don't know me one little bit," said Mr. Searle, rather shirking, I thought, the burden of this tribute and for all response to the ambiguity of the compliment.

"I should be very glad to think I didn't, sir. I've been to no small amount of personal inconvenience for you. I've pushed my way right up to the headspring. I've got the best opinion that's to be had. The best opinion that's to be had just gives you one leer over its spectacles. I guess that look will fix you if you ever get it straight. I've been able to tap, indirectly," Mr. Simmons went on, "the solicitor of your usurping cousin, and he evidently knows something to be in the wind. It seems your elder brother twenty years ago put out a feeler. So you're not to have the glory of even making them sit up."

"I never made any one sit up," I heard Mr. Searle plead. "I shouldn't begin at this time of day. I should approach the subject like a gentleman."

"Well, if you want very much to do something like a gentleman you've got a capital chance. Take your disappointment like a gentleman."

14

I had finished my dinner and had become keenly interested in poor Mr. Searle's unencouraging—or unencouraged—claim; so interested that I at last hated to hear his trouble reflected in his voice without being able—all respectfully!—to follow it in his face. I left my place, went over to the fire, took up the evening paper and established a post of observation behind it.

His cold counsellor was in the act of choosing a soft chop from the dish—an act accompanied by a great deal of prying and poking with that gentleman's own fork. My disillusioned compatriot had pushed away his plate; he sat with his elbows on the table, gloomily nursing his head with his hands. His companion watched him and then seemed to wonder—to do Mr. Simmons justice—how he could least ungracefully give him up. "I say, Searle,"—and for my benefit, I think, taking me for a native ingenuous enough to be dazzled by his wit, he lifted his voice a little and gave it an ironical ring—"in this country it's the inestimable privilege of a loyal citizen, under whatsoever stress of pleasure or of pain, to make a point of eating his dinner."

Mr. Searle gave his plate another push. "Anything may happen now. I don't care a straw."

"You ought to care. Have another chop and you WILL care. Have some better tipple. Take my advice!" Mr. Simmons went on.

My friend—I adopt that name for him—gazed from between his two hands coldly before him. "I've had enough of your advice."

"A little more," said Simmons mildly; "I shan't trouble you again. What do you mean to do?"

"Nothing."

"Oh come!"

"Nothing, nothing, nothing!"

"Nothing but starve. How about meeting expenses?"

"Why do you ask?" said my friend. "You don't care."

"My dear fellow, if you want to make me offer you twenty pounds you set most clumsily about it. You said just now I don't know you," Mr. Simmons went on. "Possibly. Come back with me then," he said kindly enough, "and let's improve our acquaintance."

"I won't go back. I shall never go back."

"Never?"

"Never."

Mr. Simmons thought it shrewdly over. "Well, you ARE sick!" he exclaimed presently. "All I can say is that if you're working out a plan for cold poison, or for any other act of desperation, you had better give it right up. You can't get a dose of the commonest kind of cold poison for nothing, you know. Look here, Searle"—and the worthy man made what struck me as a very decent appeal. "If you'll consent to return home with me by the steamer of the twenty-third I'll pay your passage down. More than that, I'll pay for your beer."

My poor gentleman met it. "I believe I never made up my mind to anything before, but I think it's made up now. I shall stay here till I take my departure for a newer world than any patched-up newness of ours. It's an odd feeling—I rather like it! What should I do at home?"

"You said just now you were homesick."

"I meant I was sick for a home. Don't I belong here? Haven't I longed to get here all my life? Haven't I counted the months and the years till I should be able to 'go' as we say? And now that I've 'gone,' that is that I've come, must I just back out? No, no, I'll move on. I'm much obliged to you for your offer. I've enough money for the present. I've about my person some forty pounds' worth of British gold, and the same amount, say, of the toughness of the heaven-sent idiot. They'll see me through together! After they're gone I shall lay my head in some English churchyard, beside some ivied tower, beneath an old gnarled black yew."

16

I had so far distinctly followed the dialogue; but at this point the landlord entered and, begging my pardon, would suggest that number 12, a most superior apartment, having now been vacated, it would give him pleasure if I would look in. I declined to look in, but agreed for number 12 at a venture and gave myself again, with dissimulation, to my friends. They had got up; Simmons had put on his overcoat; he stood polishing his rusty black hat with his napkin. "Do you mean to go down to the place?" he asked.

"Possibly. I've thought of it so often that I should like to see it."

"Shall you call on Mr. Searle?"

"Heaven forbid!"

"Something has just occurred to me," Simmons pursued with a grin that made his upper lip look more than ever denuded by the razor and jerked the ugly ornament of his chin into the air. "There's a certain Miss Searle, the old man's sister."

"Well?" my gentleman quavered.

"Well, sir!—you talk of moving on. You might move on the damsel."

Mr. Searle frowned in silence and his companion gave him a tap on the stomach. "Line those ribs a bit first!" He blushed crimson; his eyes filled with tears. "You ARE a coarse brute," he said. The scene quite harrowed me, but I was prevented from seeing it through by the reappearance of the landlord on behalf of number 12. He represented to me that I ought in justice to him to come and see how tidy they HAD made it. Half an hour afterwards I was rattling along in a hansom toward Covent Garden, where I heard Madame Bosio in The Barber of Seville. On my return from the opera I went into the coffee-room; it had occurred to me I might catch there another glimpse of Mr. Searle. I was not disappointed. I found him seated before the fire with his head sunk on his breast: he slept, dreaming perhaps of Abijah Simmons. I watched him for some moments. His closed eyes, in the dim lamplight, looked even more helpless and resigned, and I seemed to see the fine grain of his nature in his unconscious mask. They say fortune comes while we sleep, and, standing there, I felt really tender enough—though otherwise most unqualified—to be poor Mr. Searle's fortune. As I walked away I noted in one of the little prandial pews I have described the melancholy waiter, whose whiskered chin also reposed on the bulge of his shirt-front. I lingered a moment beside the old inn-yard in which, upon a time, the coaches and post-chaises found space to turn and disgorge. Above the dusky shaft of the enclosing galleries, where lounging lodgers and crumpled chambermaids and all the picturesque domesticity of a rattling tavern must have leaned on their elbows for many a year, I made out the far-off lurid twinkle of the London constellations. At the foot of the stairs, enshrined in the glittering niche of her well-appointed bar, the landlady sat napping like some solemn idol amid votive brass and plate.

The next morning, not finding the subject of my benevolent curiosity in the coffee-room, I learned from the waiter that he had ordered breakfast in bed. Into this asylum I was not yet prepared to pursue him. I spent the morning in the streets, partly under pressure of business, but catching all kinds of romantic impressions by the way. To the searching American eye there is no tint of association with which the great grimy face of London doesn't flush. As the afternoon approached, however, I began to yearn for some site more gracefully classic than what surrounded me, and, thinking over the excursions recommended to the ingenuous stranger, decided to take the train to Hampton Court. The day was the more propitious that it yielded just that dim subaqueous light which sleeps so fondly upon the English landscape.

At the end of an hour I found myself wandering through the apartments of the great palace. They follow each other in infinite succession, with no great variety of interest or aspect, but with persistent pomp and a fine specific effect. They are exactly of their various times. You pass from painted and panelled bedchambers and closets, anterooms, drawing-rooms, council-rooms, through king's suite, queen's suite, prince's suite, until you feel yourself move through the appointed hours and stages of some rigid monarchical day. On one side are the old monumental upholsteries, the big cold tarnished beds and canopies, with the circumference of disapparelled royalty symbolised by a gilded balustrade, and the great carved and yawning chimney-places where dukes-in-waiting may have warmed their weary heels; on the other, in deep recesses, rise the immense windows, the framed and draped embrasures where the sovereign whispered and favourites smiled, looking out on terraced gardens and misty park. The brown walls are dimly illumined by innumerable portraits of courtiers and captains, more especially with various members of the Batavian entourage of William of Orange, the restorer of the palace; with good store too of the lily-bosomed models of Lely and Kneller. The whole tone of this processional interior is singularly stale and sad. The tints of all things have both faded and darkened—you taste the chill of the place as you walk from room to room. It was still early in the day and in the season, and I flattered myself that I was the only visitor. This complacency, however, dropped at sight of a person standing motionless before a simpering countess of Sir Peter Lely's creation. On hearing my footstep this victim of an evaporated spell turned his head and I recognised my fellow lodger of the Red Lion. I was apparently recognised as well; he looked as if he could scarce wait for me to be kind to him, and in fact didn't wait. Seeing I had a catalogue he asked the name of the portrait. On my satisfying him he appealed, rather timidly, as to my opinion of the lady.

"Well," said I, not quite timidly enough perhaps, "I confess she strikes me as no great matter."

He remained silent and was evidently a little abashed. As we strolled away he stole a sidelong glance of farewell at his leering shepherdess. To speak with him face to face was to feel keenly that he was no less interesting than infirm. We talked of our inn, of London, of the palace; he uttered his mind freely, but seemed to struggle with a weight of depression. It was an honest mind enough, with no great cultivation but with a certain natural love of excellent things. I foresaw that I should find him quite to the manner born—to ours; full of glimpses and responses, of deserts and desolations. His perceptions would be fine and his opinions pathetic; I should moreover take refuge from his sense of proportion in his sense of humour, and then refuge from THAT, ah me!—in what? On my telling him that I was a fellow citizen he stopped short, deeply touched, and, silently passing his arm into my own, suffered me to lead him through the other apartments and down into the gardens.

A large gravelled platform stretches itself before the basement of the palace, taking the afternoon sun. Parts of the great structure are reserved for private use and habitation, occupied by state-pensioners, reduced gentlewomen in receipt of the Queen's bounty and other deserving persons. Many of the apartments have their dependent gardens, and here and there, between the verdure-coated walls, you catch a glimpse of these somewhat stuffy bowers. My companion and I measured more than once this long expanse, looking down on the floral figures of the rest of the affair and on the stoutly-woven tapestry of creeping plants that muffle the foundations of the huge red pile. I thought of the various images of old-world gentility which, early and late, must have strolled in front of it and felt the protection and security of the place. We peeped through an antique grating into one of the mossy cages and saw an old lady with a black mantilla on her head, a decanter of water in one hand and a crutch in the other, come forth, followed by three little dogs and a cat, to sprinkle a plant. She would probably have had an opinion on the virtue of Queen Caroline. Feeling these things together made us quickly, made us extraordinarily, intimate. My companion seemed to ache with his impression; he scowled, all gently, as if it gave him pain. I proposed at last that we should dine somewhere on the spot and take a late train to town. We made our way out of the gardens into the adjoining village, where we entered an inn which I pronounced, very sincerely, exactly what we wanted. Mr. Searle had approached our board as shyly as if it had been a cold bath; but, gradually warming to his work, he declared at the end of half an hour that for the first time in a month he enjoyed his victuals.

"I'm afraid you're rather out of health," I risked.

"Yes, sir—I'm an incurable."

The little village of Hampton Court stands clustered about the entrance of Bushey Park, and after we had dined we lounged along into the celebrated avenue of horse-chestnuts. There is a rare emotion, familiar to every intelligent traveller, in which the mind seems to swallow the sum total of its impressions at a gulp. You take in the whole place, whatever it be. You feel England, you feel Italy, and the sensation involves for the moment a kind of thrill. I had known it from time to time in Italy and had opened my soul to it as to the spirit of the Lord. Since my landing in England I had been waiting for it to arrive. A bottle of tolerable Burgundy, at dinner, had perhaps unlocked to it the gates of sense; it arrived now with irresistible force. Just the scene around me was the England of one's early reveries. Over against us, amid the ripeness of its gardens, the dark red residence, with its formal facings and its vacant windows, seemed to make the past definite and massive; the little village, nestling between park and palace, around a patch of turfy common, with its taverns of figurative names, its ivy-towered church, its mossy roofs, looked like the property of a feudal lord. It was in this dark composite light that I had read the British classics; it was this mild moist air that had blown from the pages of the poets; while I seemed to feel the buried generations in the dense and elastic sod. And that I must have testified in some form or other to what I have called my thrill I gather, remembering it, from a remark of my companion's.

"You've the advantage over me in coming to all this with an educated eye. You already know what old things can be. I've never known it but by report. I've always fancied I should like it. In a small way at home, of course, I did try to stand by my idea of it. I must be a conservative by nature. People at home used to call me a cockney and a fribble. But it wasn't true," he went on; "if it had been I should have made my way over here long ago: before—before—" He paused, and his head dropped sadly on his breast.

The bottle of Burgundy had loosened his tongue; I had but to choose my time for learning his story. Something told me that I had gained his confidence and that, so far as attention and attitude might go, I was "in" for responsibilities. But somehow I didn't dread them. "Before you lost your health," I suggested.

"Before I lost my health," he answered. "And my property—the little I had. And my ambition. And any power to take myself seriously."

"Come!" I cried. "You shall recover everything. This tonic English climate will wind you up in a month. And THEN see how you'll take yourself—and how I shall take you!"

"Oh," he gratefully smiled, "I may turn to dust in your hands! I should like," he presently pursued, "to be an old genteel pensioner, lodged over there in the palace and spending my days in maundering about these vistas. I should go every morning, at the hour when it gets the sun, into that long gallery where all those pretty women of Lely's are hung—I know you despise them!—and stroll up and down and say something kind to them. Poor precious forsaken creatures! So flattered and courted in their day, so neglected now! Offering up their shoulders and ringlets and smiles to that musty deadly silence!"

I laid my hand on my friend's shoulder. "Oh sir, you're all right!"

Just at this moment there came cantering down the shallow glade of the avenue a young girl on a fine black horse—one of those little budding gentlewomen, perfectly mounted and equipped, who form to alien eyes one of the prettiest incidents of English scenery. She had distanced her servant and, as she came abreast of us, turned slightly in her saddle and glanced back at him. In the movement she dropped the hunting-crop with which she was armed; whereupon she reined up and looked shyly at us and at the implement. "This is something better than a Lely," I said. Searle hastened forward, picked up the crop and, with a particular courtesy that became him handed it back to the rider. Fluttered and blushing she reached forward, took it with a quick sweet sound, and the next moment was bounding over the quiet turf. Searle stood watching her; the servant, as he passed us, touched his hat. When my friend turned toward me again I saw that he too was blushing "Oh sir, you're all right," I repeated.

At a short distance from where we had stopped was an old stone bench. We went and sat down on it and, as the sun began to sink, watched the light mist powder itself with gold. "We ought to be thinking of the train back to London, I suppose," I at last said.

"Oh hang the train!" sighed my companion.

"Willingly. There could be no better spot than this to feel the English evening stand still." So we lingered, and the twilight hung about us, strangely clear in spite of the thickness of the air. As we sat there came into view an apparition unmistakeable from afar as an immemorial vagrant—the disowned, in his own rich way, of all the English ages. As he approached us he slackened pace and finally halted, touching his cap. He was a man of middle age, clad in a greasy bonnet with false-looking ear-locks depending from its sides. Round his neck was a grimy red scarf, tucked into his waistcoat; his coat and trousers had a remote affinity with those of a reduced hostler. In one hand he had a stick; on his arm he bore a tattered basket, with a handful of withered vegetables at the bottom. His face was pale haggard and degraded beyond description—as base as a counterfeit coin, yet as modelled somehow as a tragic mask. He too, like everything else, had a history. From what height had he fallen, from what depth had he risen? He was the perfect symbol of generated constituted baseness; and I felt before him in presence of a great artist or actor.

"For God's sake, gentlemen," he said in the raucous tone of weather-beaten poverty, the tone of chronic sore-throat exacerbated by perpetual gin, "for God's sake, gentlemen, have pity on a poor fern-collector!"—turning up his stale daisies. "Food hasn't passed my lips, gentlemen, for the last three days." We gaped at him and at each other, and to our imagination his appeal had almost the force of a command. "I wonder if half-a-crown would help?" I privately wailed. And our fasting botanist went limping away through the park with the grace of controlled stupefaction still further enriching his outline.

"I feel as if I had seen my Doppelganger," said Searle. "He reminds me of myself. What am I but a mere figure in the landscape, a wandering minstrel or picker of daisies?"

"What are you 'anyway,' my friend?" I thereupon took occasion to ask. "Who are you? kindly tell me."

The colour rose again to his pale face and I feared I had offended him. He poked a moment at the sod with the point of his umbrella before answering. "Who am I?" he said at last. "My name is Clement Searle. I was born in New York, and that's the beginning and the end of me."

"Ah not the end!" I made bold to plead.

"Then it's because I HAVE no end—any more than an ill-written book. I just stop anywhere; which means I'm a failure," the poor man all lucidly and unreservedly pursued: "a failure, as hopeless and helpless, sir, as any that ever swallowed up the slender investments of the widow and the orphan. I don't pay five cents on the dollar. What I might have been—once!—there's nothing left to show. I was rotten before I was ripe. To begin with, certainly, I wasn't a fountain of wisdom. All the more reason for a definite channel—for having a little character and purpose. But I hadn't even a little. I had nothing but nice tastes, as they call them, and fine sympathies and sentiments. Take a turn through New York to-day and you'll find the tattered remnants of these things dangling on every bush and fluttering in every breeze; the men to whom I lent money, the women to whom I made love, the friends I trusted, the follies I invented, the poisonous fumes of pleasure amid which nothing was worth a thought but the manhood they stifled! It was my fault that I believed in pleasure here below. I believe in it still, but as I believe in the immortality of the soul. The soul is immortal, certainly—if you've got one; but most people haven't. Pleasure would be right if it were pleasure straight through; but it never is. My taste was to be the best in the world; well, perhaps it was. I had a little money; it went the way of my little wit. Here in my pocket I have the scant dregs of it. I should tell you I was the biggest kind of ass. Just now that description would flatter me; it would assume there's something left of me. But the ghost of a donkey—what's that? I think," he went on with a charming turn and as if striking off his real explanation, "I should have been all right in a world arranged on different lines. Before heaven, sir—whoever you are—I'm in practice so absurdly tender-hearted that I can afford to say it: I entered upon life a perfect gentleman. I had the love of old forms and pleasant rites, and I found them nowhere—found a world all hard lines and harsh lights, without shade, without composition, as they say of pictures, without the lovely mystery of colour. To furnish colour I melted down the very substance of my own soul. I went about with my brush, touching up and toning down; a very pretty chiaroscuro you'll find in my track! Sitting here in this old park, in this old country, I feel that I hover on the misty verge of what might have been! I should have been born here and not there; here my makeshift distinctions would have found things they'd have been true of.

24

How it was I never got free is more than I can say. It might have cut the knot, but the knot was too tight. I was always out of health or in debt or somehow desperately dangling. Besides, I had a horror of the great black sickening sea. A year ago I was reminded of the existence of an old claim to an English estate, which has danced before the eyes of my family, at odd moments, any time these eighty years. I confess it's a bit of a muddle and a tangle, and am by no means sure that to this hour I've got the hang of it. You look as if you had a clear head: some other time, if you consent, we'll have a go at it, such as it is, together. Poverty was staring me in the face; I sat down and tried to commit the 'points' of our case to memory, as I used to get nine-times-nine by heart as a boy. I dreamed of it for six months, half-expecting to wake up some fine morning and hear through a latticed casement the cawing of an English rookery. A couple of months ago there came out to England on business of his own a man who once got me out of a dreadful mess (not that I had hurt anyone but myself), a legal practitioner in our courts, a very rough diamond, but with a great deal of FLAIR, as they say in New York. It was with him yesterday you saw me dining. He undertook, as he called it, to 'nose round' and see if anything could be made of our questionable but possible show. The matter had never seriously been taken up. A month later I got a letter from Simmons assuring me that it seemed a very good show indeed and that he should be greatly surprised if I were unable to do something. This was the greatest push I had ever got in my life; I took a deliberate step, for the first time; I sailed for England. I've been here three days: they've seemed three months. After keeping me waiting for thirty-six hours my legal adviser makes his appearance last night and states to me, with his mouth full of mutton, that I haven't a leg to stand on, that my claim is moonshine, and that I must do penance and take a ticket for six more days of purgatory with his presence thrown in. My friend, my friend—shall I say I was disappointed? I'm already resigned. I didn't really believe I had any case. I felt in my deeper consciousness that it was the crowning illusion of a life of illusions. Well, it was a pretty one. Poor legal adviser!—I forgive him with all my heart. But for him I shouldn't be sitting in this place, in this air, under these impressions. This is a world I could have got on with beautifully. There's an immense charm in its having been kept for the last. After it nothing else would have been tolerable. I shall now have a month of it, I hope, which won't be long enough for it to "go back on me. There's one thing!"—and here, pausing, he laid his hand on mine; I rose and stood before him—"I wish it were possible you should be with me to the end."

"I promise you to leave you only when you kick me downstairs." But I suggested my terms. "It must be on condition of your omitting from your conversation this intolerable flavour of mortality. I know nothing of 'ends.' I'm all for beginnings."

He kept on me his sad weak eyes. Then with a faint smile: "Don't cut down a man you find hanging. He has had a reason for it. I'm bankrupt."

"Oh health's money!" I said. "Get well, and the rest will take care of itself. I'm interested in your questionable claim—it's the question that's the charm; and pretenders, to anything big enough, have always been, for me, an attractive class. Only their first duty's to be gallant."

"Their first duty's to understand their own points and to know their own mind," he returned with hopeless lucidity. "Don't ask me to climb our family tree now," he added; "I fear I haven't the head for it. I'll try some day—if it will bear my weight; or yours added to mine. There's no doubt, however, that we, as they say, go back. But I know nothing of business. If I were to take the matter in hand I should break in two the poor little silken thread from which everything hangs. In a better world than this I think I should be listened to. But the wind doesn't set to ideal justice. There's no doubt that a hundred years ago we suffered a palpable wrong. Yet we made no appeal at the time, and the dust of a century now lies heaped upon our silence. Let it rest!"

"What then," I asked, "is the estimated value of your interest?"

"We were instructed from the first to accept a compromise. Compared with the whole property our ideas have been small. We were once advised in the sense of a hundred and thirty thousand dollars. Why a hundred and thirty I'm sure I don't know. Don't beguile me into figures."

"Allow me one more question," I said. "Who's actually in possession?"

26

"A certain Mr. Richard Searle. I know nothing about him."

"He's in some way related to you?"

"Our great-grandfathers were half-brothers. What does that make us?"

"Twentieth cousins, say. And where does your twentieth cousin live?"

"At a place called Lackley—in Middleshire."

I thought it over. "Well, suppose we look up Lackley in Middleshire!"

He got straight up. "Go and see it?"

"Go and see it."

"Well," he said, "with you I'll go anywhere."

On our return to town we determined to spend three days there together and then proceed to our errand. We were as conscious one as the other of that deeper mystic appeal made by London to those superstitious pilgrims who feel it the mother-city of their race, the distributing heart of their traditional life. Certain characteristics of the dusky Babylon, certain aspects, phases, features, "say" more to the American spiritual ear than anything else in Europe. The influence of these things on Searle it charmed me to note. His observation I soon saw to be, as I pronounced it to him, searching and caressing. His almost morbid appetite for any over-scoring of time, well-nigh extinct from long inanition, threw the flush of its revival into his face and his talk.

II

We looked out the topography of Middleshire in a county-guide, which spoke highly, as the phrase is, of Lackley Park, and took up our abode, our journey ended, at a wayside inn where, in the days of leisure, the coach must have stopped for luncheon and burnished pewters of rustic ale been handed up as straight as possible to outsiders athirst with the sense of speed. We stopped here for mere gaping joy of its steep-thatched roof, its latticed windows, its hospitable porch, and allowed a couple of days to elapse in vague undirected strolls and sweet sentimental observance of the land before approaching the particular business that had drawn us on. The region I allude to is a compendium of the general physiognomy of England. The noble friendliness of the scenery, its latent old-friendliness, the way we scarcely knew whether we were looking at it for the first or the last time, made it arrest us at every step. The countryside, in the full warm rains of the last of April, had burst into sudden perfect spring. The dark walls of the hedgerows had turned into blooming screens, the sodden verdure of lawn and meadow been washed over with a lighter brush. We went forth without loss of time for a long walk on the great grassy hills, smooth arrested central billows of some primitive upheaval, from the summits of which you find half England unrolled at your feet. A dozen broad counties, within the scope of your vision, commingle their green exhalations. Closely beneath us lay the dark rich hedgy flats and the copse-chequered slopes, white with the blossom of apples. At widely opposite points of the expanse two great towers of cathedrals rose sharply out of a reddish blur of habitation, taking the mild English light.

We gave an irrepressible attention to this same solar reserve, and found in it only a refinement of art. The sky never was empty and never idle; the clouds were continually at play for our benefit. Over against us, from our station on the hills, we saw them piled and dissolved, condensed and shifted, blotting the blue with sullen rain-spots, stretching, breeze-fretted, into dappled fields of grey, bursting into an explosion of light or melting into a drizzle of silver. We made our way along the rounded ridge of the downs and reached, by a descent, through slanting angular fields, green to cottage-doors, a russet village that beckoned us from the heart of the maze in which the hedges wrapped it up. Close beside it, I admit, the roaring train bounces out of a hole in the hills; yet there broods upon this charming hamlet an old-time quietude that makes a violation of confidence of naming it so far away. We struck through a narrow lane, a green lane, dim with its barriers of hawthorn; it led us to a superb old farmhouse, now rather rudely jostled by the multiplied roads and by-ways that have reduced its ancient appanage. It stands there in stubborn picturesqueness, doggedly submitting to be pointed out and sketched. It is a wonderful image of the domiciliary conditions of the past—cruelly complete; with bended beams and joists, beneath the burden of gables, that seem to ache and groan with memories and regrets. The short low windows, where lead and glass combine equally to create an inward gloom, retain their opacity as a part of the primitive idea of defence. Such an old house provokes on the part of an American a luxury of respect. So propped and patched, so tinkered with clumsy tenderness, clustered so richly about its central English sturdiness, its oaken vertebrations, so humanised with ages of use and touches of beneficent affection, it seemed to offer to our grateful eyes a small rude symbol of the great English social order. Passing out upon the highroad, we came to the common browsing-patch, the "village-green" of the tales of our youth. Nothing was absent: the shaggy mouse-coloured donkey, nosing the turf with his mild and huge proboscis, the geese, the old woman—THE old woman, in person, with her red cloak and her black bonnet, frilled about the face and double-frilled beside her decent placid cheeks—the towering ploughman with his white smock-frock puckered on chest and back, his short corduroys, his mighty calves, his big red rural face. We greeted these things as children greet the loved pictures in a storybook lost and mourned and found again. We recognised them as one recognises the handwriting on letter-backs. Beside the road we saw a ploughboy straddle whistling on a stile, and he had the merit of being not only a ploughboy but a Gainsborough. Beyond the stile, across the level velvet of a meadow, a footpath wandered like a streak drawn by a finger over a surface of fine plush. We followed it from field to field and from stile to stile; it was all adorably the way to church. At the church we finally arrived, lost in its rook-haunted churchyard, hidden from the workday world by the broad stillness of pastures—a grey, grey tower, a huge black yew, a cluster of village-graves with crooked headstones and protrusions that had settled and sunk. The place seemed so to ache with consecration that my sensitive companion gave way to the force of it.

"You must bury me here, you know"—he caught at my arm. "It's the first place of worship I've seen in my life. How it makes a Sunday where it stands!"

It took the Church, we agreed, to make churches, but we had the sense the next day of seeing still better why. We walked over some seven miles, to the nearer of the two neighbouring seats of that lesson; and all through such a mist of local colour that we felt ourselves a pair of Smollett's pedestrian heroes faring tavernward for a night of adventures. As we neared the provincial city we saw the steepled mass of the cathedral, long and high, rise far into the cloud-freckled blue; and as we got closer stopped on a bridge and looked down at the reflexion of the solid minster in a yellow stream. Going further yet we entered the russet town—where surely Miss Austen's heroines, in chariots and curricles, must often have come a-shopping for their sandals and mittens; we lounged in the grassed and gravelled precinct and gazed insatiably at that most soul-soothing sight, the waning wasting afternoon light, the visible ether that feels the voices of the chimes cling far aloft to the quiet sides of the cathedral-tower; saw it linger and nestle and abide, as it loves to do on all perpendicular spaces, converting them irresistibly into registers and dials; tasted too, as deeply, of the peculiar stillness of this place of priests; saw a rosy English lad come forth and lock the door of the old foundation-school that dovetailed with cloister and choir, and carry his big responsible key into one of the quiet canonical houses: and then stood musing together on the effect on one's mind of having in one's boyhood gone and come through cathedral-shades as a King's scholar, and yet kept ruddy with much cricket in misty river meadows. On the third morning we betook ourselves to Lackley, having learned that parts of the "grounds" were open to visitors, and that indeed on application the house was sometimes shown.

30

Within the range of these numerous acres the declining spurs of the hills continued to undulate and subside. A long avenue wound and circled from the outermost gate through an untrimmed woodland, whence you glanced at further slopes and glades and copses and bosky recesses—at everything except the limits of the place. It was as free and untended as I had found a few of the large loose villas of old Italy, and I was still never to see the angular fact of English landlordism muffle itself in so many concessions. The weather had just become perfect; it was one of the dozen exquisite days of the English year—days stamped with a purity unknown in climates where fine weather is cheap. It was as if the mellow brightness, as tender as that of the primroses which starred the dark waysides like petals wind-scattered over beds of moss, had been meted out to us by the cubic foot—distilled from an alchemist's crucible. From this pastoral abundance we moved upon the more composed scene, the park proper—passed through a second lodge-gate, with weather-worn gilding on its twisted bars, to the smooth slopes where the great trees stood singly and the tame deer browsed along the bed of a woodland stream. Here before us rose the gabled grey front of the Tudor-time, developed and terraced and gardened to some later loss, as we were afterwards to know, of type.

"Here you can wander all day," I said to Searle, "like an exiled prince who has come back on tiptoe and hovers about the dominion of the usurper."

"To think of 'others' having hugged this all these years!" he answered. "I know what I am, but what might I have been? What do such places make of a man?"

"I dare say he gets stupidly used to them," I said. "But I dare say too, even then, that when you scratch the mere owner you find the perfect lover."

"What a perfect scene and background it forms!" my friend, however, had meanwhile gone on. "What legends, what histories it knows! My heart really breaks with all I seem to guess. There's Tennyson's Talking Oak! What summer days one could spend here! How I could lounge the rest of my life away on this turf of the middle ages! Haven't I some maiden-cousin in that old hall, or grange, or court—what in the name of enchantment do you call

31

the thing?—who would give me kind leave?" And then he turned almost fiercely upon me. "Why did you bring me here? Why did you drag me into this distraction of vain regrets?"

At this moment there passed within call a decent lad who had emerged from the gardens and who might have been an underling in the stables. I hailed him and put the question of our possible admittance to the house. He answered that the master was away from home, but that he thought it probable the housekeeper would consent to do the honours. I passed my arm into Searle's. "Come," I said; "drain the cup, bitter-sweet though it be. We must go in." We hastened slowly and approached the fine front. The house was one of the happiest fruits of its freshly-feeling era, a multitudinous cluster of fair gables and intricate chimneys, brave projections and quiet recesses, brown old surfaces weathered to silver and mottled roofs that testified not to seasons but to centuries. Two broad terraces commanded the wooded horizon. Our appeal was answered by a butler who condescended to our weakness. He renewed the assertion that Mr. Searle was away from home, but he would himself lay our case before the housekeeper. We would be so good, however, as to give him our cards. This request, following so directly on the assertion that Mr. Searle was absent, was rather resented by my companion. "Surely not for the housekeeper."

The butler gave a diplomatic cough. "Miss Searle is at home, sir."

"Yours alone will have to serve," said my friend. I took out a card and pencil and wrote beneath my name NEW YORK. As I stood with the pencil poised a temptation entered into it. Without in the least considering proprieties or results I let my implement yield—I added above my name that of Mr. Clement Searle. What would come of it?

Before many minutes the housekeeper waited upon us—a fresh rosy little old woman in a clean dowdy cap and a scanty sprigged gown; a quaint careful person, but accessible to the tribute of our pleasure, to say nothing of any other. She had the accent of the country, but the manners of the house. Under her guidance we passed through a dozen apartments, duly stocked with old pictures, old tapestry, old carvings, old armour, with a hundred ornaments and treasures. The pictures were especially valuable. The two Vandykes, the trio of rosy Rubenses, the sole and sombre Rembrandt, glowed with conscious authenticity. A Claude, a Murillo, a Greuze, a couple of Gainsboroughs, hung there with high complacency. Searle strolled about, scarcely speaking, pale and grave, with bloodshot eyes and lips compressed. He uttered no comment on what we saw—he asked but a question or two. Missing him at last from my side I retraced my steps and found him in a room we had just left, on a faded old ottoman and with his elbows on his knees and his face buried in his hands. Before him, ranged on a great credence, was a magnificent collection of old Italian majolica; plates of every shape, with their glaze of happy colour, jugs and vases nobly bellied and embossed. There seemed to rise before me, as I looked, a sudden vision of the young English gentleman who, eighty years ago, had travelled by slow stages to Italy and been waited on at his inn by persuasive toymen. "What is it, my dear man?" I asked. "Are you unwell?"

He uncovered his haggard face and showed me the flush of a consciousness sharper, I think, to myself than to him. "A memory of the past! There comes back to me a china vase that used to stand on the parlour mantel-shelf when I was a boy, with a portrait of General Jackson painted on one side and a bunch of flowers on the other. How long do you suppose that majolica has been in the family?"

"A long time probably. It was brought hither in the last century, into old, old England, out of old, old Italy, by some contemporary dandy with a taste for foreign gimcracks. Here it has stood for a hundred years, keeping its clear firm hues in this quiet light that has never sought to advertise it."

Searle sprang to his feet. "I say, for mercy's sake, take me away! I can't stand this sort of thing. Before I know it I shall do something scandalous. I shall steal some of their infernal crockery. I shall proclaim my identity and assert my rights. I shall go blubbering to Miss Searle and ask her in pity's name to 'put me up.'"

If he could ever have been said to threaten complications he rather visibly did so now. I began to regret my officious presentation of his name and prepared without delay to lead him out of the house. We overtook the housekeeper in the last room of the series, a small unused boudoir over whose chimney-piece hung a portrait of a young man in a powdered wig and a brocaded waistcoat. I was struck with his resemblance to my companion while our guide introduced him. "This is Mr. Clement Searle, Mr. Searle's great-uncle, by Sir Joshua Reynolds. He died young, poor gentleman; he perished at sea, going to America."

"He was the young buck who brought the majolica out of Italy," I supplemented.

"Indeed, sir, I believe he did," said the housekeeper without wonder.

"He's the image of you, my dear Searle," I further observed.

"He's remarkably like the gentleman, saving his presence," said the housekeeper.

My friend stood staring. "Clement Searle—at sea—going to America—?" he broke out. Then with some sharpness to our old woman: "Why the devil did he go to America?"

"Why indeed, sir? You may well ask. I believe he had kinsfolk there. It was for them to come to him."

Searle broke into a laugh. "It was for them to come to him! Well, well," he said, fixing his eyes on our guide, "they've come to him at last!"

She blushed like a wrinkled rose-leaf. "Indeed, sir, I verily believe you're one of US!"

"My name's the name of that beautiful youth," Searle went on. "Dear kinsman I'm happy to meet you! And what do you think of this?" he pursued as he grasped me by the arm. "I have an idea. He perished at sea. His spirit came ashore and wandered about in misery till it got another incarnation—in this poor trunk!" And he tapped his hollow chest. "Here it has rattled about these forty years, beating its wings against its rickety cage, begging to be taken home again. And I never knew what was the matter with me! Now at last the bruised spirit can escape!"

34

Our old lady gaped at a breadth of appreciation—if not at the disclosure of a connexion—beyond her. The scene was really embarrassing, and my confusion increased as we became aware of another presence. A lady had appeared in the doorway and the housekeeper dropped just audibly: "Miss Searle!" My first impression of Miss Searle was that she was neither young nor beautiful. She stood without confidence on the threshold, pale, trying to smile and twirling my card in her fingers. I immediately bowed. Searle stared at her as if one of the pictures had stepped out of its frame.

"If I'm not mistaken one of you gentlemen is Mr. Clement Searle," the lady adventured.

"My friend's Mr. Clement Searle," I took upon myself to reply. "Allow me to add that I alone am responsible for your having received his name."

"I should have been sorry not to—not to see him," said Miss Searle, beginning to blush. "Your being from America has led me—perhaps to intrude!"

"The intrusion, madam, has been on our part. And with just that excuse—that we come from so far away."

Miss Searle, while I spoke, had fixed her eyes on my friend as he stood silent beneath Sir Joshua's portrait. The housekeeper, agitated and mystified, fairly let herself go. "Heaven preserve us, Miss! It's your great-uncle's picture come to life."

"I'm not mistaken then," said Miss Searle—"we must be distantly related." She had the air of the shyest of women, for whom it was almost anguish to make an advance without help. Searle eyed her with gentle wonder from head to foot, and I could easily read his thoughts. This then was his maiden-cousin, prospective mistress of these hereditary treasures. She was of some thirty-five years of age, taller than was then common and perhaps stouter than is now enjoined. She had small kind grey eyes, a considerable quantity of very light-brown hair and a smiling well-formed mouth. She was dressed in a lustreless black satin gown with a short train. Disposed about her neck was a blue handkerchief, and over this handkerchief, in many convolutions, a string of amber beads. Her appearance was singular; she was large yet somehow vague, mature yet undeveloped. Her manner of addressing us spoke of all sorts of deep diffidences. Searle, I think, had prefigured to himself some proud cold beauty of five-and-twenty; he was relieved at finding the lady timid and not obtrusively fair. He at once had an excellent tone.

"We're distant cousins, I believe. I'm happy to claim a relationship which you're so good as to remember. I hadn't counted on your knowing anything about me."

"Perhaps I've done wrong." And Miss Searle blushed and smiled anew. "But I've always known of there being people of our blood in America, and have often wondered and asked about them—without ever learning much. To-day, when this card was brought me and I understood a Clement Searle to be under our roof as a stranger, I felt I ought to do something. But, you know, I hardly knew what. My brother's in London. I've done what I think he would have done. Welcome as a cousin." And with a resolution that ceased to be awkward she put out her hand.

"I'm welcome indeed if he would have done it half so graciously!" Again Searle, taking her hand, acquitted himself beautifully.

"You've seen what there is, I think," Miss Searle went on. "Perhaps now you'll have luncheon." We followed her into a small breakfast-room where a deep bay window opened on the mossy flags of a terrace. Here, for some moments, she remained dumb and abashed, as if resting from a measurable effort. Searle too had ceased to overflow, so that I had to relieve the silence. It was of course easy to descant on the beauties of park and mansion, and as I did so I observed our hostess. She had no arts, no impulses nor graces—scarce even any manners; she was queerly, almost frowsily dressed; yet she pleased me well. She had an antique sweetness, a homely fragrance of old traditions. To be so simple, among those complicated treasures, so pampered and yet so fresh, so modest and yet so placid, told of just the spacious leisure in which Searle and I had imagined human life to be steeped in such places as that. This figure was to the Sleeping Beauty in the Wood what a fact is to a fairy-tale, an interpretation to a myth. We, on our side, were to our hostess subjects of a curiosity not cunningly veiled.

"I should like so to go abroad!" she exclaimed suddenly, as if she meant us to take the speech for an expression of interest in ourselves.

"Have you never been?" one of us asked.

"Only once. Three years ago my brother took me to Switzerland. We thought it extremely beautiful. Except for that journey I've always lived here. I was born in this house. It's a dear old place indeed, and I know it well. Sometimes one wants a change." And on my asking her how she spent her time and what society she saw, "Of course it's very quiet," she went on, proceeding by short steps and simple statements, in the manner of a person called upon for the first time to analyse to that extent her situation. "We see very few people. I don't think there are many nice ones hereabouts. At least we don't know them. Our own family's very small. My brother cares for nothing but riding and books. He had a great sorrow ten years ago. He lost his wife and his only son, a dear little boy, who of course would have had everything. Do you know that that makes me the heir, as they've done something—I don't quite know what—to the entail? Poor old me! Since his loss my brother has preferred to be quite alone. I'm sorry he's away. But you must wait till he comes back. I expect him in a day or two." She talked more and more, as if our very strangeness led her on, about her circumstances, her solitude, her bad eyes, so that she couldn't read, her flowers, her ferns, her dogs, and the vicar, recently presented to the living by her brother and warranted quite safe, who had lately begun to light his altar candles; pausing every now and then to gasp in self-surprise, yet, in the quaintest way in the world, keeping up her story as if it were a slow rather awkward old-time dance, a difficult pas seul in which she would have been better with more practice, but of which she must complete the figure. Of all the old things I had seen in England this exhibited mind of Miss Searle's seemed to me the oldest, the most handed down and taken for granted; fenced and protected as it was by convention and precedent and usage, thoroughly acquainted with its subordinate place. I felt as if I were talking with the heroine of a last-century novel. As she talked she rested her dull eyes on her kinsman with wondering kindness. At last she put it to him: "Did you mean to go away without asking for us?"

"I had thought it over, Miss Searle, and had determined not to trouble you. You've shown me how unfriendly I should have been."

"But you knew of the place being ours, and of our relationship?"

"Just so. It was because of these things that I came down here—because of them almost that I came to England. I've always liked to think of them," said my companion.

"You merely wished to look then? We don't pretend to be much to look at."

He waited; her words were too strange. "You don't know what you are, Miss Searle."

"You like the old place then?"

Searle looked at her again in silence. "If I could only tell you!" he said at last.

"Do tell me. You must come and stay with us."

It moved him to an oddity of mirth. "Take care, take care—I should surprise you! I'm afraid I should bore you. I should never leave you."

"Oh you'd get homesick—for your real home!"

At this he was still more amused. "By the way, tell Miss Searle about our real home," he said to me. And he stepped, through the window, out upon the terrace, followed by two beautiful dogs, a setter and a young stag-hound who from the moment we came in had established the fondest relation with him. Miss Searle looked at him, while he went, as if she vaguely yearned over him; it began to be plain that she was interested in her exotic cousin. I suddenly recalled the last words I had heard spoken by my friend's adviser in London and which, in a very crude form, had reference to his making a match with this lady. If only Miss Searle could be induced to think of that, and if one had but the tact to put it in a light to her! Something assured me that her heart was virgin-soil, that the flower of romantic affection had never bloomed there. If I might just sow the seed! There seemed to shape itself within her the perfect image of one of the patient wives of old.

"He has lost his heart to England," I said. "He ought to have been born here."

"And yet he doesn't look in the least an Englishman," she still rather guardedly prosed.

"Oh it isn't his looks, poor fellow."

"Of course looks aren't everything. I never talked with a foreigner before; but he talks as I have fancied foreigners."

"Yes, he's foreign enough."

"Is he married?"

"His wife's dead and he's all alone in the world."

"Has he much property?"

"None to speak of."

"But he has means to travel."

I meditated. "He has not expected to travel far," I said at last. "You know, he's in very poor health."

"Poor gentleman! So I supposed."

"But there's more of him to go on with than he thinks. He came here because he wanted to see your place before he dies."

"Dear me—kind man!" And I imagined in the quiet eyes the hint of a possible tear. "And he was going away without my seeing him?"

"He's very modest, you see."

"He's very much the gentleman."

I couldn't but smile. "He's ALL—"

At this moment we heard on the terrace a loud harsh cry. "It's the great peacock!" said Miss Searle, stepping to the window and passing out while I followed her. Below us, leaning on the parapet, stood our appreciative friend with his arm round the neck of the setter. Before him on the grand walk strutted the familiar fowl of gardens—a splendid specimen—with ruffled neck and expanded tail. The other dog had apparently indulged in a momentary attempt to abash the gorgeous biped, but at Searle's summons had bounded back to the terrace and leaped upon the ledge, where he now stood licking his new friend's face. The scene had a beautiful old-time air: the peacock flaunting in the foreground like the genius of stately places; the broad terrace, which flattered an innate taste of mine for all deserted walks where people may have sat after heavy dinners to drink coffee in old Sevres and where the stiff brocade of women's dresses may have rustled over grass or gravel; and far around us, with one leafy circle melting into another, the timbered acres of the park. "The very beasts have made him welcome," I noted as we rejoined our companion.

"The peacock has done for you, Mr. Searle," said his cousin, "what he does only for very great people. A year ago there came here a great person—a grand old lady—to see my brother. I don't think that since then he has spread his tail as wide for any one else—not by a dozen feathers."

"It's not alone the peacock," said Searle. "Just now there came slipping across my path a little green lizard, the first I ever saw, the lizard of literature! And if you've a ghost, broad daylight though it be, I expect to see him here. Do you know the annals of your house, Miss Searle?"

"Oh dear, no! You must ask my brother for all those things."

"You ought to have a collection of legends and traditions. You ought to have loves and murders and mysteries by the roomful. I shall be ashamed of you if you haven't."

"Oh Mr. Searle! We've always been a very well-behaved family," she quite seriously pleaded. "Nothing out of the way has ever happened, I think."

"Nothing out of the way? Oh that won't do! We've managed better than that in America. Why I myself!"—and he looked at her ruefully enough, but enjoying too his idea that he might embody the social scandal or point to the darkest drama of the Searles. "Suppose I should turn out a better Searle than you—better than you nursed here in romance and extravagance? Come, don't disappoint me. You've some history among you all, you've some poetry, you've some accumulation of legend. I've been famished all my days for these things. Don't you understand? Ah you can't understand! Tell me," he rambled on, "something tremendous. When I think of what must have happened here; of the lovers who must have strolled on this terrace and wandered under the beeches, of all the figures and passions and purposes that must have haunted these walls! When I think of the births and deaths, the joys and sufferings, the young hopes and the old regrets, the rich experience of life—!" He faltered a moment with the increase of his agitation. His humour of dismay at a threat of the commonplace in the history he felt about him had turned to a deeper reaction. I began to fear however that he was really losing his head. He went on with a wilder play. "To see it all called up there before me, if the Devil alone could do it I'd make a bargain with the Devil! Ah Miss Searle," he cried, "I'm a most unhappy man!"

"Oh dear, oh dear!" she almost wailed while I turned half away.

"Look at that window, that dear little window!" I turned back to see him point to a small protruding oriel, above us, relieved against the purple brickwork, framed in chiselled stone and curtained with ivy.

"It's my little room," she said.

"Of course it's a woman's room. Think of all the dear faces—all of them so mild and yet so proud—that have looked out of that lattice, and of all the old-time women's lives whose principal view of the world has been this quiet park! Every one of them was a cousin of mine. And you, dear lady, you're one of them yet." With which he marched toward her and took her large white hand. She surrendered it, blushing to her eyes and pressing her other hand to her breast. "You're a woman of the past. You're nobly simple. It has been a romance to see you. It doesn't matter what I say to you. You didn't know me yesterday, you'll not know me to-morrow. Let me to-day do a mad sweet thing. Let me imagine in you the spirit of all the dead women who have trod the terrace-flags that lie here like sepulchral tablets in the pavement of a church. Let me say I delight in you!"—he raised her hand to his lips. She gently withdrew it and for a moment averted her face. Meeting her eyes the next instant I saw the tears had come. The Sleeping Beauty was awake.

There followed an embarrassed pause. An issue was suddenly presented by the appearance of the butler bearing a letter. "A telegram, Miss," he announced.

"Oh what shall I do?" cried Miss Searle. "I can't open a telegram. Cousin, help me."

Searle took the missive, opened it and read aloud: "I shall be home to dinner. Keep the American."

III

"KEEP the American!" Miss Searle, in compliance with the injunction conveyed in her brother's telegram (with something certainly of telegraphic curtness), lost no time in expressing the pleasure it would give her that our friend should remain. "Really you must," she said; and forthwith repaired to the house-keeper to give orders for the preparation of a room.

"But how in the world did he know of my being here?" my companion put to me.

I answered that he had probably heard from his solicitor of the other's visit. "Mr. Simmons and that gentleman must have had another interview since your arrival in England. Simmons, for reasons of his own, has made known to him your journey to this neighbourhood, and Mr. Searle, learning this, has immediately taken for granted that you've formally presented yourself to his sister. He's hospitably inclined and wishes her to do the proper thing by you. There may even," I went on, "be more in it than that. I've my little theory that he's the very phoenix of usurpers, that he has been very much struck with what the experts have had to say for you, and that he wishes to have the originality of making over to you your share—so limited after all—of the estate."

"I give it up!" my friend mused. "Come what come will!"

"You, of course," said Miss Searle, reappearing and turning to me, "are included in my brother's invitation. I've told them to see about a room for you. Your luggage shall immediately be sent for."

It was arranged that I in person should be driven over to our little inn and that I should return with our effects in time to meet Mr. Searle at dinner. On my arrival several hours later I was immediately conducted to my room. The servant pointed out to me that it communicated by a door and a private passage with that of my fellow visitor. I made my way along this passage—a low narrow corridor with a broad latticed casement through which there streamed upon a series of grotesquely sculptured oaken closets and cupboards the vivid animating glow of the western sun—knocked at his door and, getting no answer, opened it. In an armchair by the open window sat my friend asleep, his arms and legs relaxed and head dropped on his breast. It was a great relief to see him rest thus from his rhapsodies, and I watched him for some moments before waking him. There was a faint glow of colour in his cheek and a light expressive parting of his lips, something nearer to ease and peace than I had yet seen in him. It was almost happiness, it was almost health. I laid my hand on his arm and gently shook it. He opened his eyes, gazed at me a moment, vaguely recognised me, then closed them again. "Let me dream, let me dream!"

"What are you dreaming about?"

A moment passed before his answer came. "About a tall woman in a quaint black dress, with yellow hair and a sweet, sweet smile, and a soft low delicious voice! I'm in love with her."

"It's better to see her than to dream about her," I said. "Get up and dress; then we'll go down to dinner and meet her."

"Dinner—dinner—?" And he gradually opened his eyes again. "Yes, upon my word I shall dine!"

"Oh you're all right!" I declared for the twentieth time as he rose to his feet. "You'll live to bury Mr. Simmons." He told me he had spent the hours of my absence with Miss Searle—they had strolled together half over the place. "You must be very intimate," I smiled.

"She's intimate with ME. Goodness knows what rigmarole I've treated her to!" They had parted an hour ago; since when, he believed, her brother had arrived.

The slow-fading twilight was still in the great drawing-room when we came down. The housekeeper had told us this apartment was rarely used, there being others, smaller and more convenient, for the same needs. It seemed now, however, to be occupied in my comrade's honour. At the furthest end, rising to the roof like a royal tomb in a cathedral, was a great chimney-piece of chiselled white marble, yellowed by time, in which a light fire was crackling. Before the fire stood a small short man, with his hands behind him; near him was Miss Searle, so transformed by her dress that at first I scarcely knew her. There was in our entrance and reception something remarkably chilling and solemn. We moved in silence up the long room; Mr. Searle advanced slowly, a dozen steps, to meet us; his sister stood motionless. I was conscious of her masking her visage with a large white tinselled fan, and that her eyes, grave and enlarged, watched us intently over the top of it. The master of Lackley grasped in silence the proffered hand of his kinsman and eyed him from head to foot, suppressing, I noted, a start of surprise at his resemblance to Sir Joshua's portrait. "This is a happy day." And then turning to me with an odd little sharp stare: "My cousin's friend is my friend." Miss Searle lowered her fan.

The first thing that struck me in Mr. Searle's appearance was his very limited stature, which was less by half a head than that of his sister. The second was the preternatural redness of his hair and beard. They intermingled over his ears and surrounded his head like a huge lurid nimbus. His face was pale and attenuated, the face of a scholar, a dilettante, a comparer of points and texts, a man who lives in a library bending over books and prints and medals. At a distance it might have passed for smooth and rather blankly composed; but on a nearer view it revealed a number of wrinkles, sharply etched and scratched, of a singularly aged and refined effect. It was the complexion of a man of sixty. His nose was arched and delicate, identical almost with the nose of my friend. His eyes, large and deep-set, had a kind of auburn glow, the suggestion of a keen metal red-hot—or, more plainly, were full of temper and spirit. Imagine this physiognomy—grave and solemn, grotesquely solemn, in spite of the bushy brightness which made a sort of frame for it—set in motion by a queer, quick, defiant, perfunctory, preoccupied smile, and you will have an imperfect notion of the remarkable presence of our host; something better worth seeing and knowing, I perceived as I quite breathlessly took him in, than anything we had yet encountered. How thoroughly I had entered into sympathy with my poor picked-up friend, and how effectually I had associated my sensibilities with his own, I had not suspected till, within the short five minutes before the signal for dinner, I became aware, without his giving me the least hint, of his placing himself on the defensive. To neither of us was Mr. Searle sympathetic. I might have guessed from her attitude that his sister entered into our thoughts. A marked change had been wrought in her since the morning; during the hour, indeed—as I read in the light of the wondering glance he cast at her—that had elapsed since her parting with her cousin. She had not yet recovered from some great agitation. Her face was pale and she had clearly been crying. These notes of trouble gave her a new and quite perverse dignity, which was further enhanced by something complimentary and commemorative in her dress.

Whether it was taste or whether it was accident I know not; but the amiable creature, as she stood there half in the cool twilight, half in the arrested glow of the fire as it spent itself in the vastness of its marble cave, was a figure for a painter. She was habited in some faded splendour of sea-green crape and silk, a piece of millinery which, though it must have witnessed a number of dull dinners, preserved still a festive air. Over her white shoulders she wore an ancient web of the most precious and venerable lace and about her rounded throat a single series of large pearls. I went in with her to dinner, and Mr. Searle, following with my friend, took his arm, as the latter afterwards told me, and pretended jocosely to conduct him. As dinner proceeded the feeling grew within me that a drama had begun to be played in which the three persons before me were actors—each of a really arduous part. The character allotted to my friend, however, was certainly the least easy to represent with effect, though I overflowed with the desire that he should acquit himself to his honour. I seemed to see him urge his faded faculties to take their cue and perform. The poor fellow tried to do himself credit more seriously than ever in his old best days. With Miss Searle, credulous passive and pitying, he had finally flung aside all vanity and propriety and shown the bottom of his fantastic heart. But with our host there might be no talking of nonsense nor taking of liberties; there and then, if ever, sat a consummate conservative, breathing the fumes of hereditary privilege and security. For an hour, accordingly, I saw my poor protege attempt, all in pain, to meet a new decorum. He set himself the task of appearing very American, in order that his appreciation of everything Mr. Searle represented might seem purely disinterested. What his kinsman had expected him to be I know not; but

I made Mr. Searle out as annoyed, in spite of his exaggerated urbanity, at finding him so harmless. Our host was not the man to show his hand, but I think his best card had been a certain implicit confidence that so provincial a parasite would hardly have good manners.

He led the conversation to the country we had left; rather as if a leash had been attached to the collar of some lumpish and half-domesticated animal the tendency of whose movements had to be recognised. He spoke of it indeed as of some fabled planet, alien to the British orbit, lately proclaimed to have the admixture of atmospheric gases required to support animal life, but not, save under cover of a liberal afterthought, to be admitted into one's regular conception of things. I, for my part, felt nothing but regret that the spheric smoothness of his universe should be disfigured by the extrusion even of such inconsiderable particles as ourselves.

"I knew in a general way of our having somehow ramified over there," Mr. Searle mentioned; "but had scarcely followed it more than you pretend to pick up the fruit your long-armed pear tree may drop, on the other side of your wall, in your neighbour's garden. There was a man I knew at Cambridge, a very odd fellow, a decent fellow too; he and I were rather cronies; I think he afterwards went to the Middle States. They'll be, I suppose, about the Mississippi? At all events, there was that great-uncle of mine whom Sir Joshua painted. He went to America, but he never got there. He was lost at sea. You look enough like him to make one fancy he DID get there and that you've kept him alive by one of those beastly processes—I think you have 'em over there: what do you call it, 'putting up' things? If you're he you've not done a wise thing to show yourself here. He left a bad name behind him. There's a ghost who comes sobbing about the house every now and then, the ghost of one to whom he did a wrong."

"Oh mercy ON us!" cried Miss Searle in simple horror.

"Of course YOU know nothing of such things," he rather dryly allowed. "You're too sound a sleeper to hear the sobbing of ghosts."

"I'm sure I should like immensely to hear the sobbing of a ghost," said my friend, the light of his previous eagerness playing up into his eyes. "Why does it sob? I feel as if that were what we've come above all to learn."

Mr. Searle eyed his audience a moment gaugingly; he held the balance as to measure his resources. He wished to do justice to his theme. With the long finger-nails of his left hand nervously playing against the tinkling crystal of his wineglass and his conscious eyes betraying that, small and strange as he sat there, he knew himself, to his pleasure and advantage, remarkably impressive, he dropped into our untutored minds the sombre legend of his house. "Mr. Clement Searle, from all I gather, was a young man of great talents but a weak disposition. His mother was left a widow early in life, with two sons, of whom he was the elder and the more promising. She educated him with the greatest affection and care. Of course when he came to manhood she wished him to marry well. His means were quite sufficient to enable him to overlook the want of money in his wife; and Mrs. Searle selected a young lady who possessed, as she conceived, every good gift save a fortune—a fine proud handsome girl, the daughter of an old friend, an old lover I suspect, of her own. Clement, however, as it appeared, had either chosen otherwise or was as yet unprepared to choose. The young lady opened upon him in vain the battery of her attractions; in vain his mother urged her cause. Clement remained cold, insensible, inflexible. Mrs. Searle had a character which appears to have gone out of fashion in my family nowadays; she was a great manager, a maitresse-femme. A proud passionate imperious woman, she had had immense cares and ever so many law-suits; they had sharpened her temper and her will. She suspected that her son's affections had another object, and this object she began to hate. Irritated by his stubborn defiance of her wishes she persisted in her purpose. The more she watched him the more she was convinced he loved in secret. If he loved in secret of course he loved beneath him. He went about the place all sombre and sullen and brooding. At last, with the rashness of an angry woman, she threatened to bring the young lady of her choice—who, by the way, seems to have been no shrinking blossom— to stay in the house. A stormy scene was the result. He threatened that if she did so he would leave the country and sail for America. She probably disbelieved him; she knew him to be weak, but she overrated his weakness. At all events the rejected one arrived and Clement Searle departed. On a dark December day he took ship at Southampton. The two women, desperate with rage and sorrow, sat alone in this big house, mingling their tears and

48

imprecations. A fortnight later, on Christmas Eve, in the midst of a great snowstorm long famous in the country, something happened that quickened their bitterness. A young woman, battered and chilled by the storm, gained entrance to the house and, making her way into the presence of the mistress and her guest, poured out her tale. She was a poor curate's daughter out of some little hole in Gloucestershire. Clement Searle had loved her—loved her all too well! She had been turned out in wrath from her father's house; his mother at least might pity her—if not for herself then for the child she was soon to bring forth. Hut the poor girl had been a second time too trustful. The women, in scorn, in horror, with blows possibly, drove her forth again into the storm. In the storm she wandered and in the deep snow she died. Her lover, as you know, perished in that hard winter weather at sea; the news came to his mother late, but soon enough. We're haunted by the curate's daughter!"

Mr. Searle retailed this anecdote with infinite taste and point, the happiest art; when he ceased there was a pause of some moments. "Ah well we may be!" Miss Searle then mournfully murmured.

Searle blazed up into enthusiasm. "Of course, you know"—with which he began to blush violently—"I should be sorry to claim any identity with the poor devil my faithless namesake. But I should be immensely gratified if the young lady's spirit, deceived by my resemblance, were to mistake me for her cruel lover. She's welcome to the comfort of it. What one can do in the case I shall be glad to do. But can a ghost haunt a ghost? I AM a ghost!"

Mr. Searle stared a moment and then had a subtle sneer. "I could almost believe you are!"

"Oh brother—and cousin!" cried Miss Searle with the gentlest yet most appealing dignity. "How can you talk so horribly?" The horrible talk, however, evidently possessed a potent magic for my friend; and his imagination, checked a while by the influence of his kinsman, began again to lead him a dance. From this moment he ceased to steer his frail bark, to care what he said or how he said it, so long as he expressed his passionate appreciation of the scene around him. As he kept up this strain I ceased even secretly to wish he wouldn't. I have wondered since that I shouldn't have been annoyed by the way he reverted constantly to himself. But a great frankness, for the time, makes its own law and a great passion its own channel. There was moreover an irresponsible indescribable effect of beauty in everything his lips uttered. Free alike from adulation and from envy, the essence of his discourse was a divine apprehension, a romantic vision free as the flight of Ariel, of the poetry of his companions' situation and their contrasted general irresponsiveness.

"How does the look of age come?" he suddenly broke out at dessert. "Does it come of itself, unobserved, unrecorded, unmeasured? Or do you woo it and set baits and traps for it, and watch it like the dawning brownness of a meerschaum pipe, and make it fast, when it appears, just where it peeps out, and light a votive taper beneath it and give thanks to it daily? Or do you forbid it and fight it and resist it, and yet feel it settling and deepening about you as irresistible as fate?"

"What the deuce is the man talking about?" said the smile of our host.

"I found a little grey hair this morning," Miss Searle incoherently prosed.

"Well then I hope you paid it every respect!" cried her visitor.

"I looked at it for a long time in my hand-glass," she answered with more presence of mind.

"Miss Searle can for many years to come afford to be amused at grey hairs," I interposed in the hope of some greater ease. It had its effect. "Ten years from last Thursday I shall be forty-four," she almost comfortably smiled.

"Well, that's just what I am," said Searle. "If I had only come here ten years ago! I should have had more time to enjoy the feast, but I should have had less appetite. I needed first to get famished."

"Oh why did you wait for that?" his entertainer asked. "To think of these ten years that we might have been enjoying you!" At the vision of which waste and loss Mr. Searle had a fine shrill laugh.

"Well," my friend explained, "I always had a notion—a stupid vulgar notion if there ever was one—that to come abroad properly one had to have a pot of money. My pot was too nearly empty. At last I came with my empty pot!"

50

Mr. Searle had a wait for delicacy, but he proceeded. "You're reduced, you're—a—straitened?"

Our companion's very breath blew away the veil. "Reduced to nothing. Straitened to the clothes on my back!"

"You don't say so!" said Mr. Searle with a large vague gasp. "Well—well—well!" he added in a voice which might have meant everything or nothing; and then, in his whimsical way, went on to finish a glass of wine. His searching eye, as he drank, met mine, and for a moment we each rather deeply sounded the other, to the effect no doubt of a slight embarrassment. "And you," he said by way of carrying this off—"how about YOUR wardrobe?"

"Oh his!" cried my friend; "his wardrobe's immense. He could dress up a regiment!" He had drunk more champagne—I admit that the champagne was good—than was from any point of view to have been desired. He was rapidly drifting beyond any tacit dissuasion of mine. He was feverish and rash, and all attempt to direct would now simply irritate him. As we rose from the table he caught my troubled look. Passing his arm for a moment into mine, "This is the great night!" he strangely and softly said; "the night and the crisis that will settle me."

Mr. Searle had caused the whole lower portion of the house to be thrown open and a multitude of lights to be placed in convenient and effective positions. Such a marshalled wealth of ancient candlesticks and flambeaux I had never beheld. Niched against the dusky wainscots, casting great luminous circles upon the pendent stiffness of sombre tapestries, enhancing and completing with admirable effect the variety and mystery of the great ancient house, they seemed to people the wide rooms, as our little group passed slowly from one to another, with a dim expectant presence. We had thus, in spite of everything, a wonderful hour of it. Mr. Searle at once assumed the part of cicerone, and—I had not hitherto done him justice—Mr. Searle became almost agreeable. While I lingered behind with his sister he walked in advance with his kinsman. It was as if he had said: "Well, if you want the old place you shall have it—so far as the impression goes!" He spared us no thrill—I had almost said no pang—of that experience. Carrying a tall silver candlestick in his left hand, he raised it and lowered it and cast the light hither and thither, upon pictures and hangings and carvings and cornices. He knew his house to perfection. He touched upon a hundred traditions and memories, he threw off a cloud of rich reference to its earlier occupants. He threw off again, in his easy elegant way, a dozen—happily lighter—anecdotes. His relative attended with a brooding deference. Miss Searle and I meanwhile were not wholly silent.

"I suppose that by this time you and your cousin are almost old friends," I remarked.

She trifled a moment with her fan and then raised her kind small eyes. "Old friends—yet at the same time strangely new! My cousin, my cousin"— and her voice lingered on the word—"it seems so strange to call him my cousin after thinking these many years that I've no one in the world but my brother. But he's really so very odd!"

"It's not so much he as—well, as his situation, that deserves that name," I tried to reason.

"I'm so sorry for his situation. I wish I could help it in some way. He interests me so much." She gave a sweet-sounding sigh. "I wish I could have known him sooner—and better. He tells me he's but the shadow of what he used to be."

I wondered if he had been consciously practising on the sensibilities of this gentle creature. If he had I believed he had gained his point. But his position had in fact become to my sense so precarious that I hardly ventured to be glad. "His better self just now seems again to be taking shape," I said. "It will have been a good deed on your part if you help to restore him to all he ought to be."

She met my idea blankly. "Dear me, what can I do?"

"Be a friend to him. Let him like you, let him love you. I dare say you see in him now much to pity and to wonder at. But let him simply enjoy a while the grateful sense of your nearness and dearness. He'll be a better and stronger man for it, and then you can love him, you can esteem him, without restriction."

She fairly frowned for helplessness. "It's a hard part for poor stupid me to play!"

Her almost infantine innocence left me no choice but to be absolutely frank. "Did you ever play any part at all?"

She blushed as if I had been reproaching her with her insignificance. "Never! I think I've hardly lived."

"You've begun to live now perhaps. You've begun to care for something else than your old-fashioned habits. Pardon me if I seem rather meddlesome; you know we Americans are very rough and ready. It's a great moment. I wish you joy!"

"I could almost believe you're laughing at me. I feel more trouble than joy."

"Why do you feel trouble?"

She paused with her eyes fixed on our companions. "My cousin's arrival's a great disturbance," she said at last.

"You mean you did wrong in coming to meet him? In that case the fault's mine. He had no intention of giving you the opportunity."

"I certainly took too much on myself. But I can't find it in my heart to regret it. I never shall regret it! I did the only thing I COULD, heaven forgive me!"

"Heaven bless you, Miss Searle! Is any harm to come of it? I did the evil; let me bear the brunt!"

She shook her head gravely. "You don't know my brother!"

"The sooner I master the subject the better then," I said. I couldn't help relieving myself—at least by the tone of my voice—of the antipathy with which, decidedly, this gentleman had inspired me. "Not perhaps that we should get on so well together!" After which, as she turned away, "Are you VERY much afraid of him?" I added.

She gave me a shuddering sidelong glance. "He's looking at me!"

He was placed with his back to us, holding a large Venetian hand-mirror, framed in chiselled silver, which he had taken from a shelf of antiquities, just at such an angle that he caught the reflexion of his sister's person. It was evident that I too was under his attention, and was resolved I wouldn't be suspected for nothing. "Miss Searle," I said with urgency, "promise me something."

She turned upon me with a start and a look that seemed to beg me to spare her. "Oh don't ask me—please don't!" It was as if she were standing on the edge of a place where the ground had suddenly fallen away, and had been called upon to make a leap. I felt retreat was impossible, however, and that it was the greater kindness to assist her to jump.

"Promise me," I repeated.

Still with her eyes she protested. "Oh what a dreadful day!" she cried at last.

"Promise me to let him speak to you alone if he should ask you—any wish you may suspect on your brother's part notwithstanding." She coloured deeply. "You mean he has something so particular to say?"

"Something so particular!"

"Poor cousin!"

"Well, poor cousin! But promise me."

"I promise," she said, and moved away across the long room and out of the door.

"You're in time to hear the most delightful story," Searle began to me as I rejoined him and his host. They were standing before an old sombre portrait of a lady in the dress of Queen Anne's time, whose ill-painted flesh-tints showed livid, in the candle-light, against her dark drapery and background. "This is Mrs. Margaret Searle—a sort of Beatrix Esmond—qui se passait ses fantaisies. She married a paltry Frenchman, a penniless fiddler, in the teeth of her whole family. Pretty Mrs. Margaret, you must have been a woman of courage! Upon my word, she looks like Miss Searle! But pray go on. What came of it all?"

Our companion watched him with an air of distaste for his boisterous homage and of pity for his crude imagination. But he took up the tale with an effective dryness: "I found a year ago, in a box of very old papers, a letter from the lady in question to a certain Cynthia Searle, her elder sister. It was dated from Paris and dreadfully ill-spelled. It contained a most passionate appeal for pecuniary assistance. She had just had a baby, she was starving and dreadfully neglected by her husband—she cursed the day she had left England. It was a most dismal production. I never heard she found means to return."

"So much for marrying a Frenchman!" I said sententiously.

Our host had one of his waits. "This is the only lady of the family who ever was taken in by an adventurer."

"Does Miss Searle know her history?" asked my friend with a stare at the rounded whiteness of the heroine's cheek.

"Miss Searle knows nothing!" said our host with expression.

"She shall know at least the tale of Mrs. Margaret," their guest returned; and he walked rapidly away in search of her.

Mr. Searle and I pursued our march through the lighted rooms. "You've found a cousin with a vengeance," I doubtless awkwardly enough laughed.

"Ah a vengeance?" my entertainer stiffly repeated.

"I mean that he takes as keen an interest in your annals and possessions as yourself."

"Oh exactly so! He tells me he's a bad invalid," he added in a moment. "I should never have supposed it."

"Within the past few hours he's a changed man. Your beautiful house, your extreme kindness, have refreshed him immensely." Mr. Searle uttered the vague ejaculation with which self-conscious Britons so often betray the concussion of any especial courtesy of speech. But he followed this by a sudden odd glare and the sharp declaration: "I'm an honest man!" I was quite prepared to assent; but he went on with a fury of frankness, as if it were the first time in his life he had opened himself to any one, as if the process were highly disagreeable and he were hurrying through it as a task. "An honest man, mind you! I know nothing about Mr. Clement Searle! I never expected to see him. He has been to me a—a—!" And here he paused to select a word which should vividly enough express what, for good or for ill, his kinsman represented. "He has been to me an Amazement! I've no doubt he's a most amiable man. You'll not deny, however, that he's a very extraordinary sort of person. I'm sorry he's ill. I'm sorry he's poor. He's my fiftieth cousin. Well and good. I'm an honest man. He shall not have it to say that he wasn't received at my house."

"He too, thank heaven, is an honest man!" I smiled.

"Why the devil then," cried Mr. Searle, turning almost fiercely on me, "has he put forward this underhand claim to my property?"

The question, quite ringing out, flashed backward a gleam of light upon the demeanour of our host and the suppressed agitation of his sister. In an instant the jealous gentleman revealed itself. For a moment I was so surprised and scandalised at the directness of his attack that I lacked words to reply. As soon as he had spoken indeed Mr. Searle appeared to feel he had been wanting in form. "Pardon me," he began afresh, "if I speak of this matter with heat. But I've been more disgusted than I can say to hear, as I heard this morning from my solicitor, of the extraordinary proceedings of Mr. Clement Searle. Gracious goodness, sir, for what does the man take me? He pretends to the Lord knows what fantastic admiration for my place. Let him then show his respect for it by not taking too many liberties! Let him, with his high-flown parade of loyalty, imagine a tithe of what *I* feel! I love my estate; it's my passion, my conscience, my life! Am I to divide it up at this time of day with a beggarly foreigner—a man without means, without appearance, without proof, a pretender, an adventurer, a chattering mountebank? I thought America boasted having lands for all men! Upon my soul, sir, I've never been so shocked in my life."

56

I paused for some moments before speaking, to allow his passion fully to expend itself and to flicker up again if it chose; for so far as I was concerned in the whole awkward matter I but wanted to deal with him discreetly. "Your apprehensions, sir," I said at last, "your not unnatural surprise, perhaps, at the candour of our interest, have acted too much on your nerves. You're attacking a man of straw, a creature of unworthy illusion; though I'm sadly afraid you've wounded a man of spirit and conscience. Either my friend has no valid claim on your estate, in which case your agitation is superfluous; or he HAS a valid claim—"

Mr. Searle seized my arm and glared at me; his pale face paler still with the horror of my suggestion, his great eyes of alarm glowing and his strange red hair erect and quivering. "A valid claim!" he shouted. "Let him try it—let him bring it into court!"

We had emerged into the great hall and stood facing the main doorway. The door was open into the portico, through the stone archway of which I saw the garden glitter in the blue light of a full moon. As the master of the house uttered the words I have just repeated my companion came slowly up into the porch from without, bareheaded, bright in the outer moonlight, dark in the shadow of the archway, and bright again in the lamplight at the entrance of the hall. As he crossed the threshold the butler made an appearance at the head of the staircase on our left, faltering visibly a moment at sight of Mr. Searle; after which, noting my friend, he gravely descended. He bore in his hand a small silver tray. On the tray, gleaming in the light of the suspended lamp, lay a folded note. Clement Searle came forward, staring a little and startled, I think, by some quick nervous prevision of a catastrophe. The butler applied the match to the train. He advanced to my fellow visitor, all solemnly, with the offer of his missive. Mr. Searle made a movement as if to spring forward, but controlled himself. "Tottenham!" he called in a strident voice.

"Yes, sir!" said Tottenham, halting.

"Stand where you are. For whom is that note?"

"For Mr. Clement Searle," said the butler, staring straight before him and dissociating himself from everything.

"Who gave it to you?"

"Mrs. Horridge, sir." This personage, I afterwards learned, was our friend the housekeeper.

"Who gave it Mrs. Horridge?"

There was on Tottenham's part just an infinitesimal pause before replying.

"My dear sir," broke in Searle, his equilibrium, his ancient ease, completely restored by the crisis, "isn't that rather my business?"

"What happens in my house is my business, and detestable things seem to be happening." Our host, it was clear, now so furiously detested them that I was afraid he would snatch the bone of contention without more ceremony. "Bring me that thing!" he cried; on which Tottenham stiffly moved to obey.

"Really this is too much!" broke out my companion, affronted and helpless.

So indeed it struck me, and before Mr. Searle had time to take the note I possessed myself of it. "If you've no consideration for your sister let a stranger at least act for her." And I tore the disputed object into a dozen pieces.

"In the name of decency, what does this horrid business mean?" my companion quavered.

Mr. Searle was about to open fire on him, but at that moment our hostess appeared on the staircase, summoned evidently by our high-pitched contentious voices. She had exchanged her dinner-dress for a dark wrapper, removed her ornaments and begun to disarrange her hair, a thick tress of which escaped from the comb. She hurried down with a pale questioning face. Feeling distinctly that, for ourselves, immediate departure was in the air, and divining Mr. Tottenham to be a person of a few deep-seated instincts and of much latent energy, I seized the opportunity to request him, sotto voce, to send a carriage to the door without delay. "And put up our things," I added.

58

Our host rushed at his sister and grabbed the white wrist that escaped from the loose sleeve of her dress. "What was in that note?" he quite hissed at her.

Miss Searle looked first at its scattered fragments and then at her cousin. "Did you read it?"

"No, but I thank you for it!" said Searle.

Her eyes, for an instant, communicated with his own as I think they had never, never communicated with any other source of meaning; then she transferred them to her brother's face, where the sense went out of them, only to leave a dull sad patience. But there was something even in this flat humility that seemed to him to mock him, so that he flushed crimson with rage and spite and flung her away. "You always were an idiot! Go to bed."

In poor Searle's face as well the gathered serenity had been by this time all blighted and distorted and the reflected brightness of his happy day turned to blank confusion. "Have I been dealing these three hours with a madman?" he woefully cried.

"A madman, yes, if you will! A man mad with the love of his home and the sense of its stability. I've held my tongue till now, but you've been too much for me. Who the devil are you, and what and why and whence?" the terrible little man continued. "From what paradise of fools do you come that you fancy I shall make over to you, for the asking, a part of my property and my life? I'm forsooth, you ridiculous person, to go shares with you? Prove your preposterous claim! There isn't THAT in it!" And he kicked one of the bits of paper on the floor.

Searle received this broadside gaping. Then turning away he went and seated himself on a bench against the wall and rubbed his forehead amazedly. I looked at my watch and listened for the wheels of our carriage.

But his kinsman was too launched to pull himself up. "Wasn't it enough that you should have plotted against my rights? Need you have come into my very house to intrigue with my sister?"

My friend put his two hands to his face. "Oh, oh, oh!" he groaned while Miss Searle crossed rapidly and dropped on her knees at his side.

"Go to bed, you fool!" shrieked her brother.

"Dear cousin," she said, "it's cruel you're to have so to think of us!"

"Oh I shall think of YOU as you'd like!" He laid a hand on her head.

"I believe you've done nothing wrong," she brought bravely out.

"I've done what I could," Mr. Searle went on—"but it's arrant folly to pretend to friendship when this abomination lies between us. You were welcome to my meat and my wine, but I wonder you could swallow them. The sight spoiled MY appetite!" cried the master of Lackley with a laugh. "Proceed with your trumpery case! My people in London are instructed and prepared."

"I shouldn't wonder if your case had improved a good deal since you gave it up," I was moved to observe to Searle.

"Oho! you don't feign ignorance then?" and our insane entertainer shook his shining head at me. "It's very kind of you to give it up! Perhaps you'll also give up my sister!"

Searle sat staring in distress at his adversary. "Ah miserable man—I thought we had become such beautiful friends."

"Boh, you hypocrite!" screamed our host.

Searle seemed not to hear him. "Am I seriously expected," he slowly and painfully pursued, "to defend myself against the accusation of any real indelicacy—to prove I've done nothing underhand or impudent? Think what you please!" And he rose, with an effort, to his feet. "I know what YOU think!" he added to Miss Searle.

The wheels of the carriage resounded on the gravel, and at the same moment a footman descended with our two portmanteaux. Mr. Tottenham followed him with our hats and coats.

60

"Good God," our host broke out again, "you're not going away?"—an ejaculation that, after all that had happened, had the grandest comicality. "Bless my soul," he then remarked as artlessly, "of course you're going!"

"It's perhaps well," said Miss Searle with a great effort, inexpressibly touching in one for whom great efforts were visibly new and strange, "that I should tell you what my poor little note contained."

"That matter of your note, madam," her brother interrupted, "you and I will settle together!"

"Let me imagine all sorts of kind things!" Searle beautifully pleaded.

"Ah too much has been imagined!" she answered simply. "It was only a word of warning. It was to tell you to go. I knew something painful was coming."

He took his hat. "The pains and the pleasures of this day," he said to his kinsman, "I shall equally never forget. Knowing you," and he offered his hand to Miss Searle, "has been the pleasure of pleasures. I hoped something more might have come of it."

"A monstrous deal too much has come of it!" Mr. Searle irrepressibly declared.

His departing guest looked at him mildly, almost benignantly, from head to foot, and then with closed eyes and some collapse of strength, "I'm afraid so, I can't stand more," he went on. I gave him my arm and we crossed the threshold. As we passed out I heard Miss Searle break into loud weeping.

"We shall hear from each other yet, I take it!" her brother pursued, harassing our retreat.

My friend stopped, turning round on him fiercely. "You very impossible man!" he cried in his face.

"Do you mean to say you'll not prosecute?" Mr. Searle kept it up. "I shall force you to prosecute! I shall drag you into court, and you shall be beaten—beaten—beaten!" Which grim reiteration followed us on our course.

We drove of course to the little wayside inn from which we had departed in the morning so unencumbered, in all broad England, either with enemies or friends. My companion, as the carriage rolled along, seemed overwhelmed and exhausted. "What a beautiful horrible dream!" he confusedly wailed. "What a strange awakening! What a long long day! What a hideous scene! Poor me! Poor woman!" When we had resumed possession of our two little neighbouring rooms I asked him whether Miss Searle's note had been the result of anything that had passed between them on his going to rejoin her. "I found her on the terrace," he said, "walking restlessly up and down in the moonlight. I was greatly excited—I hardly know what I said. I asked her, I think, if she knew the story of Margaret Searle. She seemed frightened and troubled, and she used just the words her brother had used—'I know nothing.' For the moment, somehow, I felt as a man drunk. I stood before her and told her, with great emphasis, how poor Margaret had married a beggarly foreigner—all in obedience to her heart and in defiance to her family. As I talked the sheeted moonlight seemed to close about us, so that we stood there in a dream, in a world quite detached. She grew younger, prettier, more attractive—I found myself talking all kinds of nonsense. Before I knew it I had gone very far. I was taking her hand and calling her 'Margaret, dear Margaret!' She had said it was impossible, that she could do nothing, that she was a fool, a child, a slave. Then with a sudden sense—it was odd how it came over me there—of the reality of my connexion with the place, I spoke of my claim against the estate. 'It exists,' I declared, 'but I've given it up. Be generous! Pay me for my sacrifice.' For an instant her face was radiant. 'If I marry you,' she asked, 'will it make everything right?' Of that I at once assured her—in our marriage the whole difficulty would melt away like a rain-drop in the great sea. 'Our marriage!' she repeated in wonder; and the deep ring of her voice seemed to wake us up and show us our folly. 'I love you, but I shall never see you again,' she cried; and she hurried away with her face in her hands. I walked up and down the terrace for some moments, and then came in and met you. That's the only witchcraft I've used!"

The poor man was at once so roused and so shaken by the day's events that I believed he would get little sleep. Conscious on my own part that I shouldn't close my eyes, I but partly undressed, stirred my fire and sat down to do some writing. I heard the great clock in the little parlour below strike twelve, one, half-past one. Just as the vibration of this last stroke was dying on the air the door of communication with Searle's room was flung open and my companion stood on the threshold, pale as a corpse, in his nightshirt, shining like a phantom against the darkness behind him. "Look well at me!" he intensely gasped; "touch me, embrace me, revere me! You see a man who has seen a ghost!"

"Gracious goodness, what do you mean?"

"Write it down!" he went on. "There, take your pen. Put it into dreadful words. How do I look? Am I human? Am I pale? Am I red? Am I speaking English? A ghost, sir! Do you understand?"

I confess there came upon me by contact a kind of supernatural shock. I shall always feel by the whole communication of it that I too have seen a ghost. My first movement—I can smile at it now—was to spring to the door, close it quickly and turn the key upon the gaping blackness from which Searle had emerged. I seized his two hands; they were wet with perspiration. I pushed my chair to the fire and forced him to sit down in it; then I got on my knees and held his hands as firmly as possible. They trembled and quivered; his eyes were fixed save that the pupil dilated and contracted with extraordinary force. I asked no questions, but waited there, very curious for what he would say. At last he spoke. "I'm not frightened, but I'm—oh excited! This is life! This is living! My nerves—my heart—my brain! They're throbbing—don't you feel it? Do you tingle? Are you hot? Are you cold? Hold me tight—tight—tight! I shall tremble away into waves—into surges—and know all the secrets of things and all the reasons and all the mysteries!" He paused a moment and then went on: "A woman—as clear as that candle: no, far clearer! In a blue dress, with a black mantle on her head and a little black muff. Young and wonderfully pretty, pale and ill; with the sadness of all the women who ever loved and suffered pleading and accusing in her wet-looking eyes. God knows I never did any such thing! But she took me for my elder, for the other Clement. She came to me here as she would have come to me there. She wrung her hands and she spoke to me 'marry me!' she moaned; 'marry me

63

and put an end to my shame!' I sat up in bed, just as I sit here, looked at her, heard her—heard her voice melt away, watched her figure fade away. Bless us and save us! Here I be!"

I made no attempt either to explain or to criticise this extraordinary passage. It's enough that I yielded for the hour to the strange force of my friend's emotion. On the whole I think my own vision was the more interesting of the two. He beheld but the transient irresponsible spectre—I beheld the human subject hot from the spectral presence. Yet I soon recovered my judgement sufficiently to be moved again to try to guard him against the results of excitement and exposure. It was easily agreed that he was not for the night to return to his room, and I made him fairly comfortable in his place by my fire. Wishing above all to preserve him from a chill I removed my bedding and wrapped him in the blankets and counterpane. I had no nerves either for writing or for sleep; so I put out my lights, renewed the fuel and sat down on the opposite side of the hearth. I found it a great and high solemnity just to watch my companion. Silent, swathed and muffled to his chin, he sat rigid and erect with the dignity of his adventure. For the most part his eyes were closed; though from time to time he would open them with a steady expansion and stare, never blinking, into the flame, as if he again beheld without terror the image of the little woman with the muff. His cadaverous emaciated face, his tragic wrinkles intensified by the upward glow from the hearth, his distorted moustache, his extraordinary gravity and a certain fantastical air as the red light flickered over him, all re-enforced his fine likeness to the vision-haunted knight of La Mancha when laid up after some grand exploit. The night passed wholly without speech. Toward its close I slept for half an hour. When I awoke the awakened birds had begun to twitter and Searle, unperturbed, sat staring at me. We exchanged a long look, and I felt with a pang that his glittering eyes had tasted their last of natural sleep. "How is it? Are you comfortable?" I nevertheless asked.

He fixed me for a long time without replying and then spoke with a weak extravagance and with such pauses between his words as might have represented the slow prompting of an inner voice. "You asked me when you first knew me what I was. 'Nothing,' I said, 'nothing of any consequence.' Nothing I've always supposed myself to be. But I've wronged myself—I'm a great exception. I'm a haunted man!"

If sleep had passed out of his eyes I felt with even a deeper pang that sanity had abandoned his spirit. From this moment I was prepared for the worst. There were in my friend, however, such confirmed habits of mildness that I found myself not in the least fearing he would prove unmanageable. As morning began fully to dawn upon us I brought our curious vigil to a close. Searle was so enfeebled that I gave him my hands to help him out of his chair, and he retained them for some moments after rising to his feet, unable as he seemed to keep his balance. "Well," he said, "I've been once favoured, but don't think I shall be favoured again. I shall soon be myself as fit to 'appear' as any of them. I shall haunt the master of Lackley! It can only mean one thing—that they're getting ready for me on the other side of the grave."

When I touched the question of breakfast he replied that he had his breakfast in his pocket; and he drew from his travelling-bag a phial of morphine. He took a strong dose and went to bed. At noon I found him on foot again, dressed, shaved, much refreshed. "Poor fellow," he said, "you've got more than you bargained for—not only a man with a grievance but a man with a ghost. Well, it won't be for long!" It had of course promptly become a question whither we should now direct our steps. "As I've so little time," he argued for this, "I should like to see the best, the best alone." I answered that either for time or eternity I had always supposed Oxford to represent the English maximum, and for Oxford in the course of an hour we accordingly departed.

IV

Of that extraordinary place I shall not attempt to speak with any order or indeed with any coherence. It must ever remain one of the supreme gratifications of travel for any American aware of the ancient pieties of race. The impression it produces, the emotions it kindles in the mind of such a visitor, are too rich and various to be expressed in the halting rhythm of prose. Passing through the small oblique streets in which the long grey battered public face of the colleges seems to watch jealously for sounds that may break upon the stillness of study, you feel it the most dignified and most educated of cities. Over and through it all the great corporate fact of the University slowly throbs after the fashion of some steady bass in a concerted piece or that of the mediaeval mystical presence of the Empire in the old States of Germany. The plain perpendicular of the so mildly conventual fronts, masking blest seraglios of culture and leisure, irritates the imagination scarce less than the harem-walls of Eastern towns. Within their arching portals, however, you discover more sacred and sunless courts, and the dark verdure soothing and cooling to bookish eyes. The grey-green quadrangles stand for ever open with a trustful hospitality. The seat of the humanities is stronger in her own good manners than in a marshalled host of wardens and beadles. Directly after our arrival my friend and I wandered forth in the luminous early dusk. We reached the bridge that under-spans the walls of Magdalen and saw the eight-spired tower, delicately fluted and embossed, rise in temperate beauty—the perfect prose of Gothic—wooing the eyes to the sky that was slowly drained of day. We entered the low monkish doorway and stood in the dim little court that nestles beneath the tower, where the swallows niche more lovingly in the tangled ivy than elsewhere in Oxford, and passed into the quiet cloister and studied the small sculptured monsters on the entablature of the arcade. I rejoiced in every one of my unhappy friend's responsive vibrations, even while feeling that they might as direfully multiply as those that had preceded them. I may say that from this time forward I found it difficult to distinguish in his company between the riot of fancy and the labour of thought, or to fix the balance between what he saw and what he imagined. He had already begun playfully to exchange his identity for that of the earlier Clement Searle, and he now delivered himself almost wholly in the character of his old-time kinsman.

"THIS was my college, you know," he would almost anywhere break out, applying the words wherever we stood—"the sweetest and noblest in the whole place. How often have I strolled in this cloister with my intimates of the other world! They are all dead and buried, but many a young fellow as we meet him, dark or fair, tall or short, reminds me of the past age and the early attachment. Even as we stand here, they say, the whole thing feels about its massive base the murmurs of the tide of time; some of the foundation-stones are loosened, some of the breaches will have to be repaired. Mine was the old unregenerate Oxford, the home of rank abuses, of distinctions and privileges the most delicious and invidious. What cared I, who was a perfect gentleman and with my pockets full of money? I had an allowance of a thousand a year."

It was at once plain to me that he had lost the little that remained of his direct grasp on life and was unequal to any effort of seeing things in their order. He read my apprehension in my eyes and took pains to assure me I was right. "I'm going straight down hill. Thank heaven it's an easy slope, coated with English turf and with an English churchyard at the foot." The hysterical emotion produced by our late dire misadventure had given place to an unruffled calm in which the scene about us was reflected as in an old-fashioned mirror. We took an afternoon walk through Christ-Church meadow and at the river-bank procured a boat which I pulled down the stream to Iffley and to the slanting woods of Nuneham—the sweetest flattest reediest stream-side landscape that could be desired. Here of course we encountered the scattered phalanx of the young, the happy generation, clad in white flannel and blue, muscular fair-haired magnificent fresh, whether floated down the current by idle punts and lounging in friendly couples when not in a singleness that nursed ambitions, or straining together in rhythmic crews and hoarsely exhorted from the near bank. When to the exhibition of so much of the clearest joy of wind and limb we added the great sense of perfumed protection shed by all the enclosed lawns and groves and bowers, we felt that to be young in such scholastic shades must be a double, an infinite blessing. As my companion found himself less and less able to walk we repaired in turn to a series of gardens and spent long hours sitting in their greenest places. They struck us as the fairest things in England and the ripest and sweetest fruit of the English system. Locked in their antique verdure, guarded, as in the case of New College, by gentle battlements of silver-grey, outshouldering the matted leafage of undisseverable plants, filled with nightingales and memories, a sort of chorus of tradition; with vaguely-generous youths sprawling bookishly on the turf as if to spare it the injury of their boot-heels, and with the great conservative college countenance appealing gravely from the restless outer world, they seem places to lie down on the grass in for ever, in the happy faith that life is all a green old English garden and time an endless summer afternoon. This charmed seclusion was especially grateful to my friend, and his sense of it reached its climax, I remember, on one of the last of such occasions and while we sat in fascinated flanerie over against the sturdy back of Saint John's. The wide discreetly-windowed wall here perhaps broods upon the lawn with a more effective air of property than elsewhere. Searle dropped into fitful talk and spun his humour into golden figures. Any passing undergraduate was a peg to hang a fable, every feature of the place a pretext for more embroidery.

"Isn't it all a delightful lie?" he wanted to know. "Mightn't one fancy this the very central point of the world's heart, where all the echoes of the general life arrive but to falter and die? Doesn't one feel the air just thick with arrested voices? It's well there should be such places, shaped in the interest of factitious needs, invented to minister to the book-begotten longing for a medium in which one may dream unwaked and believe unconfuted; to foster the sweet illusion that all's well in a world where so much is so damnable, all right and rounded, smooth and fair, in this sphere of the rough and ragged, the pitiful unachieved especially, and the dreadful uncommenced. The world's made—work's over. Now for leisure! England's safe—now for Theocritus and Horace, for lawn and sky! What a sense it all gives one of the composite life of the country and of the essential furniture of its luckier minds! Thank heaven they had the wit to send me here in the other time. I'm not much visibly the braver perhaps, but think how I'm the happier! The misty spires and towers, seen far off on the level, have been all these years one of the constant things of memory. Seriously, what do the spires and towers do for these people? Are they wiser, gentler, finer, cleverer? My diminished dignity reverts in any case at moments to the naked background of our own education, the deadly dry air in which we gasp for impressions and comparisons. I assent to it all with a sort of desperate calmness; I accept it with a dogged pride. We're nursed at the opposite pole. Naked come we into a naked world. There's a certain grandeur in the lack of decorations, a certain heroic strain in that young imagination of ours which finds nothing made to its hands, which has to invent its own traditions and raise high into our morning-air, with a ringing hammer and nails, the castles in which we dwell. Noblesse oblige—Oxford must damnably do so. What a horrible thing not to rise to such examples! If you pay the pious debt to the last farthing of interest you may go through life with her blessing; but if you let it stand unhonoured you're a worse barbarian than we! But for the better or worse, in a myriad private hearts, think how she must be loved! How the youthful sentiment of mankind seems visibly to brood upon her! Think of the young lives now taking colour in her cloisters and halls. Think of the centuries' tale of dead lads—dead alike with the end of the young days to which these haunts were a present world, and the close of the larger lives which the general mother-scene has dropped into less bottomless traps. What are those two young fellows kicking their heels over on the grass there? One of them has the Saturday Review; the other—upon my soul—the other has Artemus Ward! Where do they live, how do they live, to what end do they live? Miserable boys! How can they read Artemus Ward under those windows of Elizabeth? What do you think loveliest in all Oxford? The poetry of certain windows. Do you see that one yonder, the second of those lesser bays, with the broken cornice and the lattice? That used to be the window of my bosom friend a hundred years ago. Remind me to tell you the story of that broken cornice. Don't pretend it's not a common thing to have one's bosom friend at another college. Pray was I committed to common things? He was a charming fellow. By the way, he was a good deal like you. Of course his cocked hat, his long hair in a black ribbon, his cinnamon velvet suit and his flowered waistcoat made a difference. We gentlemen used to wear swords."

69

There was really the touch of grace in my poor friend's divagations—the disheartened dandy had so positively turned rhapsodist and seer. I was particularly struck with his having laid aside the diffidence and self-consciousness of the first days of our acquaintance. He had become by this time a disembodied observer and critic; the shell of sense, growing daily thinner and more transparent, transmitted the tremor of his quickened spirit. He seemed to pick up acquaintances, in the course of our contemplations, merely by putting out his hand. If I left him for ten minutes I was sure to find him on my return in earnest conversation with some affable wandering scholar. Several young men with whom he had thus established relations invited him to their rooms and entertained him, as I gathered, with rather rash hospitality. For myself, I chose not to be present at these symposia; I shrank partly from being held in any degree responsible for his extravagance, partly from the pang of seeing him yield to champagne and an admiring circle. He reported such adventures with less keen a complacency than I had supposed he might use, but a certain method in his madness, a certain dignity in his desire to fraternise, appeared to save him from mischance. If they didn't think him a harmless lunatic they certainly thought him a celebrity of the Occident. Two things, however, grew evident—that he drank deeper than was good for him and that the flagrant freshness of his young patrons rather interfered with his predetermined sense of the element of finer romance. At the same time it completed his knowledge of the place. Making the acquaintance of several tutors and fellows, he dined in hall in half a dozen colleges, alluding afterwards to these banquets with religious unction. One evening after a participation indiscreetly prolonged he came back to the hotel in a cab, accompanied by a friendly undergraduate and a physician and looking deadly pale. He had swooned away on leaving table and remained so rigidly unconscious as much to agitate his banqueters. The following twenty-four hours he of course spent in bed, but on the third day declared himself strong enough to begin afresh. On his reaching the street his strength once more forsook him, so that I insisted on his returning to his room. He besought me with tears in his eyes not to shut him up. "It's my last chance—I want to go back for an hour to that garden of Saint John's. Let me eat and drink—to-morrow I die." It seemed to me possible that with a Bath-chair the expedition might be accomplished.

The hotel, it appeared, possessed such a convenience, which was immediately produced. It became necessary hereupon that we should have a person to propel the chair. As there was no one on the spot at liberty I was about to perform the office; but just as my patient had got seated and wrapped—he now had a perpetual chill—an elderly man emerged from a lurking-place near the door and, with a formal salute, offered to wait upon the gentleman. We assented, and he proceeded solemnly to trundle the chair before him. I recognised him as a vague personage whom I had observed to lounge shyly about the doors of the hotels, at intervals during our stay, with a depressed air of wanting employment and a poor semblance of finding it. He had once indeed in a half-hearted way proposed himself as an amateur cicerone for a tour through the colleges; and I now, as I looked at him, remembered with a pang that I had too curtly declined his ministrations. Since then his shyness, apparently, had grown less or his misery greater, for it was with a strange grim avidity that he now attached himself to our service. He was a pitiful image of shabby gentility and the dinginess of "reduced circumstances." He would have been, I suppose, some fifty years of age; but his pale haggard unwholesome visage, his plaintive drooping carriage and the irremediable disarray of his apparel seemed to add to the burden of his days and tribulations. His eyes were weak and bloodshot, his bold nose was sadly compromised, and his reddish beard, largely streaked with grey, bristled under a month's neglect of the razor. In all this rusty forlornness lurked a visible assurance of our friend's having known better days. Obviously he was the victim of some fatal depreciation in the market value of pure gentility. There had been something terribly affecting in the way he substituted for the attempt to touch the greasy rim of his antiquated hat some such bow as one man of the world might make another. Exchanging a few words with him as we went I was struck with the decorum of his accent. His fine whole voice should have been congruously cracked.

"Take me by some long roundabout way," said Searle, "so that I may see as many college-walls as possible."

"You know," I asked of our attendant, "all these wonderful ins and outs?"

"I ought to, sir," he said, after a moment, with pregnant gravity. And as we were passing one of the colleges, "That used to be my place," he added.

At these words Searle desired him to stop and come round within sight. "You say that's YOUR college?"

"The place might deny me, sir; but heaven forbid I should seem to take it ill of her. If you'll allow me to wheel you into the quad I'll show you my windows of thirty years ago."

Searle sat staring, his huge pale eyes, which now left nothing else worth mentioning in his wasted face, filled with wonder and pity. "If you'll be so kind," he said with great deference. But just as this perverted product of a liberal education was about to propel him across the threshold of the court he turned about, disengaged the mercenary hands, with one of his own, from the back of the chair, drew their owner alongside and turned to me. "While we're here, my dear fellow," he said, "be so good as to perform this service. You understand?" I gave our companion a glance of intelligence and we resumed our way. The latter showed us his window of the better time, where a rosy youth in a scarlet smoking-fez now puffed a cigarette at the open casement. Thence we proceeded into the small garden, the smallest, I believe, and certainly the sweetest, of all the planted places of Oxford. I pushed the chair along to a bench on the lawn, turned it round, toward the front of the college and sat down by it on the grass. Our attendant shifted mournfully from one foot to the other, his patron eyeing him open-mouthed. At length Searle broke out: "God bless my soul, sir, you don't suppose I expect you to stand! There's an empty bench."

"Thank you," said our friend, who bent his joints to sit.

"You English are really fabulous! I don't know whether I most admire or most abominate you! Now tell me: who are you? what are you? what brought you to this?"

The poor fellow blushed up to his eyes, took off his hat and wiped his forehead with an indescribable fabric drawn from his pocket. "My name's Rawson, sir. Beyond that it's a long story."

"I ask out of sympathy," said Searle. "I've a fellow-feeling. If you're a poor devil I'm a poor devil as well."

"I'm the poorer devil of the two," said the stranger with an assurance for once presumptuous.

"Possibly. I suppose an English poor devil's the poorest of all poor devils. And then you've fallen from a height. From a gentleman commoner—is that what they called you?—to a propeller of Bath-chairs. Good heavens, man, the fall's enough to kill you!"

"I didn't take it all at once, sir. I dropped a bit one time and a bit another."

"That's me, that's me!" cried Searle with all his seriousness.

"And now," said our friend, "I believe I can't drop any further."

"My dear fellow"—and Searle clasped his hand and shook it—"I too am at the very bottom of the hole."

Mr. Rawson lifted his eyebrows. "Well, sir, there's a difference between sitting in such a pleasant convenience and just trudging behind it!"

"Yes—there's a shade. But I'm at my last gasp, Mr. Rawson."

"I'm at my last penny, sir."

"Literally, Mr. Rawson?"

Mr. Rawson shook his head with large loose bitterness. "I've almost come to the point of drinking my beer and buttoning my coat figuratively; but I don't talk in figures."

Fearing the conversation might appear to achieve something like gaiety at the expense of Mr. Rawson's troubles, I took the liberty of asking him, with all consideration, how he made a living.

"I don't make a living," he answered with tearful eyes; "I can't make a living. I've a wife and three children—and all starving, sir. You wouldn't believe what I've come to. I sent my wife to her mother's, who can ill afford to keep her, and came to Oxford a week ago, thinking I might pick up a few half-crowns by showing people about the colleges. But it's no use. I haven't the assurance. I don't look decent. They want a nice little old man with black gloves and a clean shirt and a silver-headed stick. What do I look as if I knew about Oxford, sir?"

"Mercy on us," cried Searle, "why didn't you speak to us before?"

"I wanted to; half a dozen times I've been on the point of it. I knew you were Americans."

"And Americans are rich!" cried Searle, laughing. "My dear Mr. Rawson, American as I am I'm living on charity."

"And I'm exactly not, sir! There it is. I'm dying for the lack of that same. You say you're a pauper, but it takes an American pauper to go bowling about in a Bath-chair. America's an easy country."

"Ah me!" groaned Searle. "Have I come to the most delicious corner of the ancient world to hear the praise of Yankeeland?"

"Delicious corners are very well, and so is the ancient world," said Mr. Rawson; "but one may sit here hungry and shabby, so long as one isn't too shabby, as well as elsewhere. You'll not persuade me that it's not an easier thing to keep afloat yonder than here. I wish *I* were in Yankeeland, that's all!" he added with feeble force. Then brooding for a moment on his wrongs: "Have you a bloated brother? or you, sir? It matters little to you. But it has mattered to me with a vengeance! Shabby as I sit here I can boast that advantage—as he his five thousand a year. Being but a twelvemonth my elder he swaggers while I go thus. There's old England for you! A very pretty place for HIM!"

"Poor old England!" said Searle softly.

"Has your brother never helped you?" I asked.

"A five-pound note now and then! Oh I don't say there haven't been times when I haven't inspired an irresistible sympathy. I've not been what I should. I married dreadfully out of the way. But the devil of it is that he started fair and I started foul; with the tastes, the desires, the needs, the sensibilities of a gentleman—and not another blessed 'tip.' I can't afford to live in England."

"THIS poor gentleman fancied a couple of months ago that he couldn't afford to live in America," I fondly explained.

"I'd 'swap'—do you call it?—chances with him!" And Mr. Rawson looked quaintly rueful over his freedom of speech.

Searle sat supported there with his eyes closed and his face twitching for violent emotion, and then of a sudden had a glare of gravity. "My friend, you're a dead failure! Be judged! Don't talk about 'swapping.' Don't talk about chances. Don't talk about fair starts and false starts. I'm at that point myself that I've a right to speak. It lies neither in one's chance nor one's start to make one a success; nor in anything one's brother—however bloated—can do or can undo. It lies in one's character. You and I, sir, have HAD no character—that's very plain. We've been weak, sir; as weak as water. Here we are for it—sitting staring in each other's faces and reading our weakness in each other's eyes. We're of no importance whatever, Mr. Rawson!"

Mr. Rawson received this sally with a countenance in which abject submission to the particular affirmed truth struggled with the comparative propriety of his general rebellion against fate. In the course of a minute a due self-respect yielded to the warm comfortable sense of his being relieved of the cares of an attitude. "Go on, sir, go on," he said. "It's wholesome doctrine." And he wiped his eyes with what seemed his sole remnant of linen.

"Dear, dear," sighed Searle, "I've made you cry! Well, we speak as from man to man. I should be glad to think you had felt for a moment the side-light of that great undarkening of the spirit which precedes—which precedes the grand illumination of death."

Mr. Rawson sat silent a little, his eyes fixed on the ground and his well-cut nose but the more deeply dyed by his agitation. Then at last looking up: "You're a very good-natured man, sir, and you'll never persuade me you don't come of a kindly race. Say what you please about a chance; when a man's fifty—degraded, penniless, a husband and father—a chance to get on his legs again is not to be despised. Something tells me that my luck may be in your country—which has brought luck to so many. I can come on the parish here of course, but I don't want to come on the parish. Hang it, sir, I want to hold up my head. I see thirty years of life before me yet. If only by God's help I could have a real change of air! It's a fixed idea of mine. I've had it for the last ten years. It's not that I'm a low radical. Oh I've no vulgar opinions. Old England's good enough for me, but I'm not good enough for old England. I'm a shabby man that wants to get out of a room full of staring gentlefolk. I'm for ever put to the blush. It's a perfect agony of spirit; everything reminds me of my younger and better self. The thing for me would be a cooling cleansing plunge into the unknowing and the unknown! I lie awake thinking of it."

Searle closed his eyes, shivering with a long-drawn tremor which I hardly knew whether to take for an expression of physical or of mental pain. In a moment I saw it was neither. "Oh my country, my country, my country!" he murmured in a broken voice; and then sat for some time abstracted and lost. I signalled our companion that it was time we should bring our small session to a close, and he, without hesitating, possessed himself of the handle of the Bath-chair and pushed it before him. We had got halfway home before Searle spoke or moved. Suddenly in the High Street, as we passed a chop-house from whose open doors we caught a waft of old-fashioned cookery and other restorative elements, he motioned us to halt. "This is my last five pounds"— and he drew a note from his pocket-book. "Do me the favour, Mr. Rawson, to accept it. Go in there and order the best dinner they can give you. Call for a bottle of Burgundy and drink it to my eternal rest!"

Mr. Rawson stiffened himself up and received the gift with fingers momentarily irresponsive. But Mr. Rawson had the nerves of a gentleman. I measured the spasm with which his poor dispossessed hand closed upon the crisp paper, I observed his empurpled nostril convulsive under the other solicitation. He crushed the crackling note in his palm with a passionate pressure and jerked a spasmodic bow. "I shall not do you the wrong, sir, of anything but the best!" The next moment the door swung behind him.

Searle sank again into his apathy, and on reaching the hotel I helped him to get to bed. For the rest of the day he lay without motion or sound and beyond reach of any appeal. The doctor, whom I had constantly in attendance, was sure his end was near. He expressed great surprise that he should have lasted so long; he must have been living for a month on the very dregs of his strength. Toward evening, as I sat by his bedside in the deepening dusk, he roused himself with a purpose I had vaguely felt gathering beneath his stupor.

"My cousin, my cousin," he said confusedly. "Is she here?" It was the first time he had spoken of Miss Searle since our retreat from her brother's house, and he continued to ramble. "I was to have married her. What a dream! That day was like a string of verses—rhymed hours. But the last verse is bad measure. What's the rhyme to 'love'? ABOVE! Was she a simple woman, a kind sweet woman? Or have I only dreamed it? She had the healing gift; her touch would have cured my madness. I want you to do something. Write three lines, three words: 'Good-bye; remember me; be happy.'" And then after a long pause: "It's strange a person in my state should have a wish. Why should one eat one's breakfast the day one's hanged? What a creature is man! What a farce is life! Here I lie, worn down to a mere throbbing fever-point; I breathe and nothing more, and yet I DESIRE! My desire lives. If I could see her! Help me out with it and let me die."

Half an hour later, at a venture, I dispatched by post a note to Miss Searle: "Your cousin is rapidly sinking. He asks to see you." I was conscious of a certain want of consideration in this act, since it would bring her great trouble and yet no power to face the trouble; but out of her distress I fondly hoped a sufficient force might be born. On the following day my friend's exhaustion had become so great that I began to fear his intelligence altogether broken up. But toward evening he briefly rallied, to maunder about many things, confounding in a sinister jumble the memories of the past weeks and those of bygone years. "By the way," he said suddenly, "I've made no will. I haven't much to bequeath. Yet I have something." He had been playing listlessly with a large signet-ring on his left hand, which he now tried to draw off. "I leave you this"—working it round and round vainly—"if you can get it off. What enormous knuckles! There must be such knuckles in the mummies of the Pharaohs. Well, when I'm gone—! No, I leave you something more precious than gold—the sense of a great kindness. But I've a little gold left. Bring me those trinkets." I placed on the bed before him several articles of jewellery, relics of early foppery: his watch and chain, of great value, a locket and seal, some odds and ends of goldsmith's work. He trifled with them feebly for some moments, murmuring various names and dates associated with them. At last, looking up with clearer interest, "What has become," he asked, "of Mr. Rawson?"

"You want to see him?"

"How much are these things worth?" he went on without heeding me. "How much would they bring?" And he weighed them in his weak hands. "They're pretty heavy. Some hundred or so? Oh I'm richer than I thought! Rawson—Rawson—you want to get out of this awful England?"

I stepped to the door and requested the servant whom I kept in constant attendance in our adjacent sitting-room to send and ascertain if Mr. Rawson were on the premises. He returned in a few moments, introducing our dismal friend. Mr. Rawson was pale even to his nose and derived from his unaffectedly concerned state an air of some distinction. I led him up to the bed. In Searle's eyes, as they fell on him, there shone for a moment the light of a human message.

"Lord have mercy!" gasped Mr. Rawson.

"My friend," said Searle, "there's to be one American the less—so let there be at the same time one the more. At the worst you'll be as good a one as I. Foolish me! Take these battered relics; you can sell them; let them help you on your way. They're gifts and mementoes, but this is a better use. Heaven speed you! May America be kind to you. Be kind, at the last, to your own country!"

"Really this is too much; I can't," the poor man protested, almost scared and with tears in his eyes. "Do come round and get well and I'll stop here. I'll stay with you and wait on you."

"No, I'm booked for my journey, you for yours. I hope you don't mind the voyage."

Mr. Rawson exhaled a groan of helpless gratitude, appealing piteously from so strange a windfall. "It's like the angel of the Lord who bids people in the Bible to rise and flee!"

Searle had sunk back upon his pillow, quite used up; I led Mr. Rawson back into the sitting-room, where in three words I proposed to him a rough valuation of our friend's trinkets. He assented with perfect good-breeding; they passed into my possession and a second bank-note into his.

From the collapse into which this wondrous exercise of his imagination had plunged him my charge then gave few signs of being likely to emerge. He breathed, as he had said, and nothing more. The twilight deepened; I lighted the night-lamp. The doctor sat silent and official at the foot of the bed; I resumed my constant place near the head. Suddenly our patient opened his eyes wide. "She'll not come," he murmured. "Amen! she's an English sister." Five minutes passed; he started forward. "She's come, she's here!" he confidently quavered. His words conveyed to my mind so absolute an assurance that I lightly rose and passed into the sitting-room. At the same moment, through the opposite door, the servant introduced a lady. A lady, I say; for an instant she was simply such—tall pale dressed in deep mourning. The next instant I had uttered her name—"Miss Searle!" She looked ten years older.

She met me with both hands extended and an immense question in her face. "He has just announced you," I said. And then with a fuller consciousness of the change in her dress and countenance: "What has happened?"

"Oh death, death!" she wailed. "You and I are left."

There came to me with her words a sickening shock, the sense of poetic justice somehow cheated, defeated. "Your brother?" I panted.

She laid her hand on my arm and I felt its pressure deepen as she spoke. "He was thrown from his horse in the park. He died on the spot. Six days have passed. Six months!"

She accepted my support and a moment later we had entered the room and approached the bedside, from which the doctor withdrew. Searle opened his eyes and looked at her from head to foot. Suddenly he seemed to make out her mourning. "Already!" he cried audibly and with a smile, as I felt, of pleasure.

She dropped on her knees and took his hand. "Not for you, cousin," she whispered. "For my poor brother."

He started, in all his deathly longitude, as with a galvanic shock. "Dead! HE dead! Life itself!" And then after a moment and with a slight rising inflexion: "You're free?"

"Free, cousin. Too sadly free. And now—NOW—with what use for freedom?"

He looked steadily into her eyes, dark in the heavy shadow of her musty mourning-veil. "For me wear colours!"

In a moment more death had come, the doctor had silently attested it, and she had burst into sobs.

We buried him in the little churchyard in which he had expressed the wish to lie; beneath one of the blackest and widest of English yews and the little tower than which none in all England has a softer and hoarier grey. A year has passed; Miss Searle, I believe, has begun to wear colours.

About Author

Henry James OM (15 April 1843 – 28 February 1916) was an American-British author regarded as a key transitional figure between literary realism and literary modernism, and is considered by many to be among the greatest novelists in the English language. He was the son of Henry James Sr. and the brother of renowned philosopher and psychologist William James and diarist Alice James.

He is best known for a number of novels dealing with the social and marital interplay between émigré Americans, English people, and continental Europeans. Examples of such novels include The Portrait of a Lady, The Ambassadors, and The Wings of the Dove. His later works were increasingly experimental. In describing the internal states of mind and social dynamics of his characters, James often made use of a style in which ambiguous or contradictory motives and impressions were overlaid or juxtaposed in the discussion of a character's psyche. For their unique ambiguity, as well as for other aspects of their composition, his late works have been compared to impressionist painting.

His novella The Turn of the Screw has garnered a reputation as the most analysed and ambiguous ghost story in the English language and remains his most widely adapted work in other media. He also wrote a number of other highly regarded ghost stories and is considered one of the greatest masters of the field.

James published articles and books of criticism, travel, biography, autobiography, and plays. Born in the United States, James largely relocated to Europe as a young man and eventually settled in England, becoming a British subject in 1915, one year before his death. James was nominated for the Nobel Prize in Literature in 1911, 1912 and 1916.

Life

Early years, 1843–1883

James was born at 2 Washington Place in New York City on 15 April 1843. His parents were Mary Walsh and Henry James Sr. His father was intelligent and steadfastly congenial. He was a lecturer and philosopher who had inherited independent means from his father, an Albany banker and investor. Mary came from a wealthy family long settled in New York City. Her sister Katherine lived with her adult family for an extended period of time. Henry Jr. had three brothers, William, who was one year his senior, and younger brothers Wilkinson (Wilkie) and Robertson. His younger sister was Alice. Both of his parents were of Irish and Scottish descent.

The family first lived in Albany, at 70 N. Pearl St., and then moved to Fourteenth Street in New York City when James was still a young boy. His education was calculated by his father to expose him to many influences, primarily scientific and philosophical; it was described by Percy Lubbock, the editor of his selected letters, as "extraordinarily haphazard and promiscuous." James did not share the usual education in Latin and Greek classics. Between 1855 and 1860, the James' household traveled to London, Paris, Geneva, Boulogne-sur-Mer and Newport, Rhode Island, according to the father's current interests and publishing ventures, retreating to the United States when funds were low. Henry studied primarily with tutors and briefly attended schools while the family traveled in Europe. Their longest stays were in France, where Henry began to feel at home and became fluent in French. He was afflicted with a stutter, which seems to have manifested itself only when he spoke English; in French, he did not stutter.

In 1860 the family returned to Newport. There Henry became a friend of the painter John La Farge, who introduced him to French literature, and in particular, to Balzac. James later called Balzac his "greatest master," and said that he had learned more about the craft of fiction from him than from anyone else.

In the autumn of 1861 Henry received an injury, probably to his back, while fighting a fire. This injury, which resurfaced at times throughout his life, made him unfit for military service in the American Civil War.

84

In 1864 the James family moved to Boston, Massachusetts to be near William, who had enrolled first in the Lawrence Scientific School at Harvard and then in the medical school. In 1862 Henry attended Harvard Law School, but realised that he was not interested in studying law. He pursued his interest in literature and associated with authors and critics William Dean Howells and Charles Eliot Norton in Boston and Cambridge, formed lifelong friendships with Oliver Wendell Holmes Jr., the future Supreme Court Justice, and with James and Annie Fields, his first professional mentors.

His first published work was a review of a stage performance, "Miss Maggie Mitchell in Fanchon the Cricket," published in 1863. About a year later, A Tragedy of Error, his first short story, was published anonymously. James's first payment was for an appreciation of Sir Walter Scott's novels, written for the North American Review. He wrote fiction and non-fiction pieces for The Nation and Atlantic Monthly, where Fields was editor. In 1871 he published his first novel, Watch and Ward, in serial form in the Atlantic Monthly. The novel was later published in book form in 1878.

During a 14-month trip through Europe in 1869–70 he met Ruskin, Dickens, Matthew Arnold, William Morris, and George Eliot. Rome impressed him profoundly. "Here I am then in the Eternal City," he wrote to his brother William. "At last—for the first time—I live!" He attempted to support himself as a freelance writer in Rome, then secured a position as Paris correspondent for the New York Tribune, through the influence of its editor John Hay. When these efforts failed he returned to New York City. During 1874 and 1875 he published Transatlantic Sketches, A Passionate Pilgrim, and Roderick Hudson. During this early period in his career he was influenced by Nathaniel Hawthorne.

In 1869 he settled in London. There he established relationships with Macmillan and other publishers, who paid for serial installments that they would later publish in book form. The audience for these serialized novels was largely made up of middle-class women, and James struggled to fashion serious literary work within the strictures imposed by editors' and publishers' notions of what was suitable for young women to read. He lived in rented rooms but was able to join gentlemen's clubs that had libraries and where he could entertain male friends. He was introduced to English society by Henry Adams and Charles Milnes Gaskell, the latter introducing him to the Travellers' and the Reform Clubs.

In the fall of 1875 he moved to the Latin Quarter of Paris. Aside from two trips to America, he spent the next three decades—the rest of his life—in Europe. In Paris he met Zola, Alphonse Daudet, Maupassant, Turgenev, and others. He stayed in Paris only a year before moving to London.

In England he met the leading figures of politics and culture. He continued to be a prolific writer, producing The American (1877), The Europeans (1878), a revision of Watch and Ward (1878), French Poets and Novelists (1878), Hawthorne (1879), and several shorter works of fiction. In 1878 Daisy Miller established his fame on both sides of the Atlantic. It drew notice perhaps mostly because it depicted a woman whose behavior is outside the social norms of Europe. He also began his first masterpiece, The Portrait of a Lady, which would appear in 1881.

In 1877 he first visited Wenlock Abbey in Shropshire, home of his friend Charles Milnes Gaskell whom he had met through Henry Adams. He was much inspired by the darkly romantic Abbey and the surrounding countryside, which features in his essay Abbeys and Castles. In particular the gloomy monastic fishponds behind the Abbey are said to have inspired the lake in The Turn of the Screw.

While living in London, James continued to follow the careers of the "French realists", Émile Zola in particular. Their stylistic methods influenced his own work in the years to come. Hawthorne's influence on him faded during this period, replaced by George Eliot and Ivan Turgenev. 1879–1882 saw the publication of The Europeans, Washington Square, Confidence, and The Portrait of a Lady. He visited America in 1882–1883, then returned to London.

The period from 1881 to 1883 was marked by several losses. His mother died in 1881, followed by his father a few months later, and then by his brother Wilkie. Emerson, an old family friend, died in 1882. His friend Turgenev died in 1883.

Middle years, 1884–1897

In 1884 James made another visit to Paris. There he met again with Zola, Daudet, and Goncourt. He had been following the careers of the French "realist" or "naturalist" writers, and was increasingly influenced by them. In 1886, he published The Bostonians and The Princess Casamassima, both influenced by the French writers he'd studied assiduously. Critical reaction and sales were poor. He wrote to Howells that the books had hurt his career rather than helped because they had "reduced the desire, and demand, for my productions to zero". During this time he became friends with Robert Louis Stevenson, John Singer Sargent, Edmund Gosse, George du Maurier, Paul Bourget, and Constance Fenimore Woolson. His third novel from the 1880s was The Tragic Muse. Although he was following the precepts of Zola in his novels of the '80s, their tone and attitude are closer to the fiction of Alphonse Daudet. The lack of critical and financial success for his novels during this period led him to try writing for the theatre. (His dramatic works and his experiences with theatre are discussed below.)

In the last quarter of 1889, he started translating "for pure and copious lucre" Port Tarascon, the third volume of Alphonse Daudet adventures of Tartarin de Tarascon. Serialized in Harper's Monthly Magazine from June 1890, this translation praised as "clever" by The Spectator was published in January 1891 by Sampson Low, Marston, Searle & Rivington.

After the stage failure of Guy Domville in 1895, James was near despair and thoughts of death plagued him. The years spent on dramatic works were not entirely a loss. As he moved into the last phase of his career he found ways to adapt dramatic techniques into the novel form.

In the late 1880s and throughout the 1890s James made several trips through Europe. He spent a long stay in Italy in 1887. In that year the short novel The Aspern Papers and The Reverberator were published.

Late years, 1898–1916

In 1897–1898 he moved to Rye, Sussex, and wrote The Turn of the Screw. 1899–1900 saw the publication of The Awkward Age and The Sacred

Fount. During 1902–1904 he wrote The Ambassadors, The Wings of the Dove, and The Golden Bowl.

In 1904 he revisited America and lectured on Balzac. In 1906–1910 he published The American Scene and edited the "New York Edition", a 24-volume collection of his works. In 1910 his brother William died; Henry had just joined William from an unsuccessful search for relief in Europe on what then turned out to be his (Henry's) last visit to the United States (from summer 1910 to July 1911), and was near him, according to a letter he wrote, when he died.

In 1913 he wrote his autobiographies, A Small Boy and Others, and Notes of a Son and Brother. After the outbreak of the First World War in 1914 he did war work. In 1915 he became a British subject and was awarded the Order of Merit the following year. He died on 28 February 1916, in Chelsea, London. As he requested, his ashes were buried in Cambridge Cemetery in Massachusetts.

Biographers

James regularly rejected suggestions that he should marry, and after settling in London proclaimed himself "a bachelor". F. W. Dupee, in several volumes on the James family, originated the theory that he had been in love with his cousin Mary ("Minnie") Temple, but that a neurotic fear of sex kept him from admitting such affections: "James's invalidism ... was itself the symptom of some fear of or scruple against sexual love on his part." Dupee used an episode from James's memoir A Small Boy and Others, recounting a dream of a Napoleonic image in the Louvre, to exemplify James's romanticism about Europe, a Napoleonic fantasy into which he fled.

Dupee had not had access to the James family papers and worked principally from James's published memoir of his older brother, William, and the limited collection of letters edited by Percy Lubbock, heavily weighted toward James's last years. His account therefore moved directly from James's childhood, when he trailed after his older brother, to elderly invalidism. As more material became available to scholars, including the diaries of contemporaries and hundreds of affectionate and sometimes erotic letters

88

written by James to younger men, the picture of neurotic celibacy gave way to a portrait of a closeted homosexual.

Between 1953 and 1972, Leon Edel authored a major five-volume biography of James, which accessed unpublished letters and documents after Edel gained the permission of James's family. Edel's portrayal of James included the suggestion he was celibate. It was a view first propounded by critic Saul Rosenzweig in 1943. In 1996 Sheldon M. Novick published Henry James: The Young Master, followed by Henry James: The Mature Master (2007). The first book "caused something of an uproar in Jamesian circles" as it challenged the previous received notion of celibacy, a once-familiar paradigm in biographies of homosexuals when direct evidence was non-existent. Novick also criticised Edel for following the discounted Freudian interpretation of homosexuality "as a kind of failure." The difference of opinion erupted in a series of exchanges between Edel and Novick which were published by the online magazine Slate, with the latter arguing that even the suggestion of celibacy went against James's own injunction "live!"—not "fantasize!"

A letter James wrote in old age to Hugh Walpole has been cited as an explicit statement of this. Walpole confessed to him of indulging in "high jinks", and James wrote a reply endorsing it: "We must know, as much as possible, in our beautiful art, yours & mine, what we are talking about — & the only way to know it is to have lived & loved & cursed & floundered & enjoyed & suffered — I don't think I regret a single 'excess' of my responsive youth".

The interpretation of James as living a less austere emotional life has been subsequently explored by other scholars. The often intense politics of Jamesian scholarship has also been the subject of studies. Author Colm Tóibín has said that Eve Kosofsky Sedgwick's Epistemology of the Closet made a landmark difference to Jamesian scholarship by arguing that he be read as a homosexual writer whose desire to keep his sexuality a secret shaped his layered style and dramatic artistry. According to Tóibín such a reading "removed James from the realm of dead white males who wrote about posh people. He became our contemporary."

James's letters to expatriate American sculptor Hendrik Christian Andersen have attracted particular attention. James met the 27-year-old Andersen in Rome in 1899, when James was 56, and wrote letters to Andersen that are intensely emotional: "I hold you, dearest boy, in my innermost love, & count on your feeling me—in every throb of your soul". In a letter of 6 May 1904, to his brother William, James referred to himself as "always your hopelessly celibate even though sexagenarian Henry". How accurate that description might have been is the subject of contention among James's biographers, but the letters to Andersen were occasionally quasi-erotic: "I put, my dear boy, my arm around you, & feel the pulsation, thereby, as it were, of our excellent future & your admirable endowment." To his homosexual friend Howard Sturgis, James could write: "I repeat, almost to indiscretion, that I could live with you. Meanwhile I can only try to live without you."

His numerous letters to the many young gay men among his close male friends are more forthcoming. In a letter to Howard Sturgis, following a long visit, James refers jocularly to their "happy little congress of two" and in letters to Hugh Walpole he pursues convoluted jokes and puns about their relationship, referring to himself as an elephant who "paws you oh so benevolently" and winds about Walpole his "well meaning old trunk". His letters to Walter Berry printed by the Black Sun Press have long been celebrated for their lightly veiled eroticism.

He corresponded in almost equally extravagant language with his many female friends, writing, for example, to fellow novelist Lucy Clifford: "Dearest Lucy! What shall I say? when I love you so very, very much, and see you nine times for once that I see Others! Therefore I think that—if you want it made clear to the meanest intelligence—I love you more than I love Others." To his New York friend Mary Cadwalader Jones: "Dearest Mary Cadwalader. I yearn over you, but I yearn in vain; & your long silence really breaks my heart, mystifies, depresses, almost alarms me, to the point even of making me wonder if poor unconscious & doting old Célimare [Jones's pet name for James] has 'done' anything, in some dark somnambulism of the spirit, which has ... given you a bad moment, or a wrong impression, or a 'colourable pretext' ... However these things may be, he loves you as tenderly as ever;

nothing, to the end of time, will ever detach him from you, & he remembers those Eleventh St. matutinal intimes hours, those telephonic matinées, as the most romantic of his life ..." His long friendship with American novelist Constance Fenimore Woolson, in whose house he lived for a number of weeks in Italy in 1887, and his shock and grief over her suicide in 1894, are discussed in detail in Edel's biography and play a central role in a study by Lyndall Gordon. (Edel conjectured that Woolson was in love with James and killed herself in part because of his coldness, but Woolson's biographers have objected to Edel's account.)

Works

Style and themes

James is one of the major figures of trans-Atlantic literature. His works frequently juxtapose characters from the Old World (Europe), embodying a feudal civilisation that is beautiful, often corrupt, and alluring, and from the New World (United States), where people are often brash, open, and assertive and embody the virtues—freedom and a more highly evolved moral character—of the new American society. James explores this clash of personalities and cultures, in stories of personal relationships in which power is exercised well or badly. His protagonists were often young American women facing oppression or abuse, and as his secretary Theodora Bosanquet remarked in her monograph Henry James at Work:

> When he walked out of the refuge of his study and into the world and looked around him, he saw a place of torment, where creatures of prey perpetually thrust their claws into the quivering flesh of doomed, defenseless children of light ... His novels are a repeated exposure of this wickedness, a reiterated and passionate plea for the fullest freedom of development, unimperiled by reckless and barbarous stupidity.

Critics have jokingly described three phases in the development of James's prose: "James I, James II, and The Old Pretender." He wrote short stories and plays. Finally, in his third and last period he returned to the long, serialised novel. Beginning in the second period, but most noticeably in the third, he increasingly abandoned direct statement in favour of frequent double negatives, and complex descriptive imagery. Single paragraphs began to run for page after page, in which an initial noun would be succeeded by pronouns surrounded by clouds of adjectives and prepositional clauses, far from their original referents, and verbs would be deferred and then preceded by a series of adverbs. The overall effect could be a vivid evocation of a scene as perceived by a sensitive observer. It has been debated whether this change of style was engendered by James's shifting from writing to dictating to a typist, a change made during the composition of What Maisie Knew.

In its intense focus on the consciousness of his major characters, James's later work foreshadows extensive developments in 20th century fiction. Indeed, he might have influenced stream-of-consciousness writers such as Virginia Woolf, who not only read some of his novels but also wrote essays about them. Both contemporary and modern readers have found the late style difficult and unnecessary; his friend Edith Wharton, who admired him greatly, said that there were passages in his work that were all but incomprehensible. James was harshly portrayed by H. G. Wells as a hippopotamus laboriously attempting to pick up a pea that had got into a corner of its cage. The "late James" style was ably parodied by Max Beerbohm in "The Mote in the Middle Distance".

More important for his work overall may have been his position as an expatriate, and in other ways an outsider, living in Europe. While he came from middle-class and provincial beginnings (seen from the perspective of European polite society) he worked very hard to gain access to all levels of society, and the settings of his fiction range from working class to aristocratic, and often describe the efforts of middle-class Americans to make their way in European capitals. He confessed he got some of his best story ideas from gossip at the dinner table or at country house weekends. He worked for a living, however, and lacked the experiences of select schools, university, and army service, the common bonds of masculine society. He was furthermore a man whose tastes and interests were, according to the prevailing standards of Victorian era Anglo-American culture, rather feminine, and who was shadowed by the cloud of prejudice that then and later accompanied suspicions of his homosexuality. Edmund Wilson famously compared James's objectivity to Shakespeare's:

One would be in a position to appreciate James better if one compared him with the dramatists of the seventeenth century—Racine and Molière, whom he resembles in form as well as in point of view, and even Shakespeare, when allowances are made for the most extreme differences in subject and form. These poets are not, like Dickens and Hardy, writers of melodrama—either humorous or pessimistic, nor secretaries of society like Balzac, nor prophets like Tolstoy: they are occupied simply with the presentation of conflicts of moral character, which they do not concern themselves about softening or averting. They do not indict society for these situations: they regard them as universal and inevitable. They do not even blame God for allowing them: they accept them as the conditions of life.

It is also possible to see many of James's stories as psychological thought-experiments. In his preface to the New York edition of The American he describes the development of the story in his mind as exactly such: the "situation" of an American, "some robust but insidiously beguiled and betrayed, some cruelly wronged, compatriot..." with the focus of the story being on the response of this wronged man. The Portrait of a Lady may be an experiment to see what happens when an idealistic young woman suddenly becomes very rich. In many of his tales, characters seem to exemplify alternative futures and possibilities, as most markedly in "The Jolly Corner", in which the protagonist and a ghost-doppelganger live alternative American and European lives; and in others, like The Ambassadors, an older James seems fondly to regard his own younger self facing a crucial moment.

Major novels

The first period of James's fiction, usually considered to have culminated in The Portrait of a Lady, concentrated on the contrast between Europe and America. The style of these novels is generally straightforward and, though personally characteristic, well within the norms of 19th-century fiction. Roderick Hudson (1875) is a Künstlerroman that traces the development of the title character, an extremely talented sculptor. Although the book shows some signs of immaturity—this was James's first serious attempt at a full-length novel—it has attracted favourable comment due to the vivid realisation of the three major characters: Roderick Hudson, superbly gifted but unstable and unreliable; Rowland Mallet, Roderick's limited but much more mature friend and patron; and Christina Light, one of James's most enchanting and maddening femmes fatales. The pair of Hudson and Mallet has been seen as representing the two sides of James's own nature: the wildly imaginative artist and the brooding conscientious mentor.

In The Portrait of a Lady (1881) James concluded the first phase of his career with a novel that remains his most popular piece of long fiction. The story is of a spirited young American woman, Isabel Archer, who "affronts her destiny" and finds it overwhelming. She inherits a large amount of money and subsequently becomes the victim of Machiavellian scheming by two American expatriates. The narrative is set mainly in Europe, especially in England and Italy. Generally regarded as the masterpiece of his early phase, The Portrait of a Lady is described as a psychological novel, exploring the minds of his characters, and almost a work of social science, exploring the differences between Europeans and Americans, the old and the new worlds.

The second period of James's career, which extends from the publication of The Portrait of a Lady through the end of the nineteenth century, features less popular novels including The Princess Casamassima, published serially in The Atlantic Monthly in 1885–1886, and The Bostonians, published serially in The Century Magazine during the same period. This period also featured James's celebrated Gothic novella, The Turn of the Screw.

The third period of James's career reached its most significant achievement in three novels published just around the start of the 20th century: The Wings of the Dove (1902), The Ambassadors (1903), and The Golden Bowl (1904). Critic F. O. Matthiessen called this "trilogy" James's major phase, and these novels have certainly received intense critical study. It was the second-written of the books, The Wings of the Dove (1902) that was the first published because it attracted no serialization. This novel tells the story of Milly Theale, an American heiress stricken with a serious disease, and her impact on the people around her. Some of these people befriend Milly with honourable motives, while others are more self-interested. James stated in his autobiographical books that Milly was based on Minny Temple, his beloved cousin who died at an early age of tuberculosis. He said that he attempted in the novel to wrap her memory in the "beauty and dignity of art".

Shorter narratives

James was particularly interested in what he called the "beautiful and blest nouvelle", or the longer form of short narrative. Still, he produced a number of very short stories in which he achieved notable compression of sometimes complex subjects. The following narratives are representative of James's achievement in the shorter forms of fiction.

- "A Tragedy of Error" (1864), short story

- "The Story of a Year" (1865), short story

- A Passionate Pilgrim (1871), novella

- Madame de Mauves (1874), novella

- Daisy Miller (1878), novella

- The Aspern Papers (1888), novella

- The Lesson of the Master (1888), novella

- The Pupil (1891), short story

- "The Figure in the Carpet" (1896), short story

- The Beast in the Jungle (1903), novella

- An International Episode (1878)

- Picture and Text

- Four Meetings (1885)

- A London Life, and Other Tales (1889)

- The Spoils of Poynton (1896)

- Embarrassments (1896)
- The Two Magics: The Turn of the Screw, Covering End (1898)
- A Little Tour of France (1900)
- The Sacred Fount (1901)
- Views and Reviews (1908)
- The Wings of the Dove, Volume I (1902)
- The Wings of the Dove, Volume II (1909)
- The Finer Grain (1910)
- The Outcry (1911)
- Lady Barbarina: The Siege of London, An International Episode and Other Tales (1922)
- The Birthplace (1922)

Plays

At several points in his career James wrote plays, beginning with one-act plays written for periodicals in 1869 and 1871 and a dramatisation of his popular novella Daisy Miller in 1882. From 1890 to 1892, having received a bequest that freed him from magazine publication, he made a strenuous effort to succeed on the London stage, writing a half-dozen plays of which only one, a dramatisation of his novel The American, was produced. This play was performed for several years by a touring repertory company and had a respectable run in London, but did not earn very much money for James. His other plays written at this time were not produced.

In 1893, however, he responded to a request from actor-manager George Alexander for a serious play for the opening of his renovated St. James's Theatre, and wrote a long drama, Guy Domville, which Alexander produced. There was a noisy uproar on the opening night, 5 January 1895, with hissing from the gallery when James took his bow after the final curtain, and the author was upset. The play received moderately good reviews and had a modest run of four weeks before being taken off to make way for Oscar Wilde's The Importance of Being Earnest, which Alexander thought would have better prospects for the coming season.

After the stresses and disappointment of these efforts James insisted that he would write no more for the theatre, but within weeks had agreed to write a curtain-raiser for Ellen Terry. This became the one-act "Summersoft", which he later rewrote into a short story, "Covering End", and then expanded into a full-length play, The High Bid, which had a brief run in London in 1907, when James made another concerted effort to write for the stage. He wrote three new plays, two of which were in production when the death of Edward VII on 6 May 1910 plunged London into mourning and theatres closed. Discouraged by failing health and the stresses of theatrical work, James did not renew his efforts in the theatre, but recycled his plays as successful novels. The Outcry was a best-seller in the United States when it was published in 1911. During the years 1890–1893 when he was most engaged with the theatre, James wrote a good deal of theatrical criticism and assisted Elizabeth Robins and others in translating and producing Henrik Ibsen for the first time in London.

Leon Edel argued in his psychoanalytic biography that James was traumatised by the opening night uproar that greeted Guy Domville, and that it plunged him into a prolonged depression. The successful later novels, in Edel's view, were the result of a kind of self-analysis, expressed in fiction, which partly freed him from his fears. Other biographers and scholars have not accepted this account, however; the more common view being that of F.O. Matthiessen, who wrote: "Instead of being crushed by the collapse of his hopes [for the theatre]... he felt a resurgence of new energy."

Non-fiction

Beyond his fiction, James was one of the more important literary critics in the history of the novel. In his classic essay The Art of Fiction (1884), he argued against rigid prescriptions on the novelist's choice of subject and method of treatment. He maintained that the widest possible freedom in content and approach would help ensure narrative fiction's continued vitality.

James wrote many valuable critical articles on other novelists; typical is his book-length study of Nathaniel Hawthorne, which has been the subject of critical debate. Richard Brodhead has suggested that the study was emblematic of James's struggle with Hawthorne's influence, and constituted an effort to place the elder writer "at a disadvantage." Gordon Fraser, meanwhile, has suggested that the study was part of a more commercial effort by James to introduce himself to British readers as Hawthorne's natural successor.

When James assembled the New York Edition of his fiction in his final years, he wrote a series of prefaces that subjected his own work to searching, occasionally harsh criticism.

At 22 James wrote The Noble School of Fiction for The Nation's first issue in 1865. He would write, in all, over 200 essays and book, art, and theatre reviews for the magazine.

For most of his life James harboured ambitions for success as a playwright. He converted his novel The American into a play that enjoyed modest returns in the early 1890s. In all he wrote about a dozen plays, most of which went unproduced. His costume drama Guy Domville failed disastrously on its opening night in 1895. James then largely abandoned his efforts to conquer the stage and returned to his fiction. In his Notebooks he maintained that his theatrical experiment benefited his novels and tales by helping him dramatise his characters' thoughts and emotions. James produced a small but valuable amount of theatrical criticism, including perceptive appreciations of Henrik Ibsen.

With his wide-ranging artistic interests, James occasionally wrote on the visual arts. Perhaps his most valuable contribution was his favourable assessment of fellow expatriate John Singer Sargent, a painter whose critical status has improved markedly in recent decades. James also wrote sometimes charming, sometimes brooding articles about various places he visited and lived in. His most famous books of travel writing include Italian Hours (an example of the charming approach) and The American Scene (most definitely on the brooding side).

James was one of the great letter-writers of any era. More than ten thousand of his personal letters are extant, and over three thousand have been published in a large number of collections. A complete edition of James's letters began publication in 2006, edited by Pierre Walker and Greg Zacharias. As of 2014, eight volumes have been published, covering the period from 1855 to 1880. James's correspondents included celebrated contemporaries like Robert Louis Stevenson, Edith Wharton and Joseph Conrad, along with many others in his wide circle of friends and acquaintances. The letters range from the "mere twaddle of graciousness" to serious discussions of artistic, social and personal issues.

Very late in life James began a series of autobiographical works: A Small Boy and Others, Notes of a Son and Brother, and the unfinished The Middle Years. These books portray the development of a classic observer who was passionately interested in artistic creation but was somewhat reticent about participating fully in the life around him.

Reception

Criticism, biographies and fictional treatments

James's work has remained steadily popular with the limited audience of educated readers to whom he spoke during his lifetime, and has remained firmly in the canon, but, after his death, some American critics, such as Van Wyck Brooks, expressed hostility towards James for his long expatriation and eventual naturalisation as a British subject. Other critics such as E. M. Forster complained about what they saw as James's squeamishness in the treatment of sex and other possibly controversial material, or dismissed his late style as difficult and obscure, relying heavily on extremely long sentences and excessively latinate language. Similarly Oscar Wilde criticised him for writing "fiction as if it were a painful duty". Vernon Parrington, composing a canon of American literature, condemned James for having cut himself off from America. Jorge Luis Borges wrote about him, "Despite the scruples and delicate complexities of James, his work suffers from a major defect: the absence of life." And Virginia Woolf, writing to Lytton Strachey, asked, "Please tell me what you find in Henry James. ... we have his works here, and

I read, and I can't find anything but faintly tinged rose water, urbane and sleek, but vulgar and pale as Walter Lamb. Is there really any sense in it?" The novelist W. Somerset Maugham wrote, "He did not know the English as an Englishman instinctively knows them and so his English characters never to my mind quite ring true," and argued "The great novelists, even in seclusion, have lived life passionately. Henry James was content to observe it from a window." Maugham nevertheless wrote, "The fact remains that those last novels of his, notwithstanding their unreality, make all other novels, except the very best, unreadable." Colm Tóibín observed that James "never really wrote about the English very well. His English characters don't work for me."

Despite these criticisms, James is now valued for his psychological and moral realism, his masterful creation of character, his low-key but playful humour, and his assured command of the language. In his 1983 book, The Novels of Henry James, Edward Wagenknecht offers an assessment that echoes Theodora Bosanquet's:

> "To be completely great," Henry James wrote in an early review, "a work of art must lift up the heart," and his own novels do this to an outstanding degree ... More than sixty years after his death, the great novelist who sometimes professed to have no opinions stands foursquare in the great Christian humanistic and democratic tradition. The men and women who, at the height of World War II, raided the secondhand shops for his out-of-print books knew what they were about. For no writer ever raised a braver banner to which all who love freedom might adhere.

William Dean Howells saw James as a representative of a new realist school of literary art which broke with the English romantic tradition epitomised by the works of Charles Dickens and William Makepeace Thackeray. Howells wrote that realism found "its chief exemplar in Mr. James... A novelist he is not, after the old fashion, or after any fashion but his own." F.R. Leavis championed Henry James as a novelist of "established pre-eminence" in The Great Tradition (1948), asserting that The Portrait of a Lady and The Bostonians were "the two most brilliant novels in the language." James is now prized as a master of point of view who moved literary fiction forward by insisting in showing, not telling, his stories to the reader. (Source: Wikipedia)

NOTABLE WORKS

NOVELS

Watch and Ward (1871)

Roderick Hudson (1875)

The American (1877)

The Europeans (1878)

Confidence (1879)

Washington Square (1880)

The Portrait of a Lady (1881)

The Bostonians (1886)

The Princess Casamassima (1886)

The Reverberator (1888)

The Tragic Muse (1890)

The Other House (1896)

The Spoils of Poynton (1897)

What Maisie Knew (1897)

The Awkward Age (1899)

The Sacred Fount (1901)

The Wings of the Dove (1902)

The Ambassadors (1903)

The Golden Bowl (1904)

The Whole Family (collaborative novel with eleven other authors, 1908)

The Outcry (1911)

The Ivory Tower (unfinished, published posthumously 1917)

The Sense of the Past (unfinished, published posthumously 1917)

SHORT STORIES AND NOVELLAS

A Tragedy of Error (1864)

The Story of a Year (1865)

A Landscape Painter (1866)

A Day of Days (1866)

My Friend Bingham (1867)

Poor Richard (1867)

The Story of a Masterpiece (1868)

A Most Extraordinary Case (1868)

A Problem (1868)

De Grey: A Romance (1868)

Osborne's Revenge (1868)

The Romance of Certain Old Clothes (1868)

A Light Man (1869)

Gabrielle de Bergerac (1869)

Travelling Companions (1870)

A Passionate Pilgrim (1871)

At Isella (1871)

Master Eustace (1871)

Guest's Confession (1872)

The Madonna of the Future (1873)

The Sweetheart of M. Briseux (1873)

The Last of the Valerii (1874)

Madame de Mauves (1874)

Adina (1874)

Professor Fargo (1874)

Eugene Pickering (1874)

Benvolio (1875)

Crawford's Consistency (1876)

The Ghostly Rental (1876)

Four Meetings (1877)

Rose-Agathe (1878, as Théodolinde)

Daisy Miller (1878)

Longstaff's Marriage (1878)

An International Episode (1878)

The Pension Beaurepas (1879)

A Diary of a Man of Fifty (1879)

A Bundle of Letters (1879)

The Point of View (1882)

The Siege of London (1883)

Impressions of a Cousin (1883)

Lady Barberina (1884)

Pandora (1884)

The Author of Beltraffio (1884)

Georgina's Reasons (1884)

A New England Winter (1884)

The Path of Duty (1884)

Mrs. Temperly (1887)

Louisa Pallant (1888)

The Aspern Papers (1888)

The Liar (1888)

The Modern Warning (1888, originally published as The Two Countries)

A London Life (1888)

The Patagonia (1888)

The Lesson of the Master (1888)

The Solution (1888)

The Pupil (1891)

Brooksmith (1891)

The Marriages (1891)

The Chaperon (1891)

Sir Edmund Orme (1891)

Nona Vincent (1892)

The Real Thing (1892)

The Private Life (1892)

Lord Beaupré (1892)

The Visits (1892)

Sir Dominick Ferrand (1892)

Greville Fane (1892)

Collaboration (1892)

Owen Wingrave (1892)

The Wheel of Time (1892)

The Middle Years (1893)

The Death of the Lion (1894)

The Coxon Fund (1894)

The Next Time (1895)

Glasses (1896)

The Altar of the Dead (1895)

The Figure in the Carpet (1896)

The Way It Came (1896, also published as The Friends of the Friends)

The Turn of the Screw (1898)

Covering End (1898)

In the Cage (1898)

John Delavoy (1898)

The Given Case (1898)

Europe (1899)

The Great Condition (1899)

The Real Right Thing (1899)

Paste (1899)

The Great Good Place (1900)

Maud-Evelyn (1900)

Miss Gunton of Poughkeepsie (1900)

The Tree of Knowledge (1900)

The Abasement of the Northmores (1900)

The Third Person (1900)

The Special Type (1900)

The Tone of Time (1900)

Broken Wings (1900)

The Two Faces (1900)

Mrs. Medwin (1901)

The Beldonald Holbein (1901)

The Story in It (1902)

Flickerbridge (1902)

The Birthplace (1903)

The Beast in the Jungle (1903)

The Papers (1903)

Fordham Castle (1904)

Julia Bride (1908)

The Jolly Corner (1908)

The Velvet Glove (1909)

Mora Montravers (1909)

Crapy Cornelia (1909)

The Bench of Desolation (1909)

A Round of Visits (1910)

OTHER

Transatlantic Sketches (1875)

French Poets and Novelists (1878)

Hawthorne (1879)

Portraits of Places (1883)

A Little Tour in France (1884)

Partial Portraits (1888)

Essays in London and Elsewhere (1893)

Picture and Text (1893)

Terminations (1893)

Theatricals (1894)

Theatricals: Second Series (1895)

Guy Domville (1895)

The Soft Side (1900)

William Wetmore Story and His Friends (1903)

The Better Sort (1903)

English Hours (1905)

The Question of our Speech; The Lesson of Balzac. Two Lectures (1905)

The American Scene (1907)

Views and Reviews (1908)

Italian Hours (1909)

A Small Boy and Others (1913)

Notes on Novelists (1914)

Notes of a Son and Brother (1914)

Within the Rim (1918)

Travelling Companions (1919)

Notebooks (various, published posthumously)

The Middle Years (unfinished, published posthumously 1917)

A Most Unholy Trade (1925, published posthumously)

The Art of the Novel : Critical Prefaces (1934)

CPSIA information can be obtained
at www.ICGtesting.com
Printed in the USA
LVHW111757050920
665176LV00006B/109